CONTENTS

Case of the Ostentatious Otters

Book 8

J.M. POOLE

Secret Staircase Books

Case of the Ostentatious Otters

Corgi Case Files, Book 8

By

J.M. Poole
www.AuthorJMPoole.com

A corgi sploot is highly contagious.

Case of the Ostentatious Otters
Published by Secret Staircase Books, an imprint of
Columbine Publishing Group, LLC
PO Box 416, Angel Fire, NM 87710

Book layout and design by Secret Staircase Books
Cover images © Felipe de Barros, J.M. Poole, Yevgen Kachurin, Papapishu

First Secret Staircase paperback edition: January 2021
First Secret Staircase e-book edition: January 2021

Publisher's Cataloging-in-Publication Data

Poole, J.M.
Case of the Ostentatious Otters / by J.M. Poole.
p. cm.
ISBN 978-1649140333 (paperback)
ISBN 978-1649140340 (e-book)

1. Zachary Anderson (Fictitious character)--Fiction. 2. Pomme Valley, Oregon—Fiction. 3. Monterey Bay Aquarium—Fiction. 4. Corgi dogs—Fiction. 5. Amateur sleuth—Fiction. I. Title

Corgi Case Files mystery series : Book 8.
Poole, J.M., Corgi Case Files mysteries.

BISAC : FICTION / Mystery & Detective.

813/.54

ACKNOWLEDGMENTS

This book was written in a (for me) amazingly short amount of time. As such, there are always a list of people to thank for bringing everything together. Of course, there's Giliane, my wife. How she puts up with me on a day to day basis is a mystery, no doubt about it. Maybe it's because she knows she's stuck with me? :)

Then there are the members of my Posse, who willingly accepted my preposterous demands and – grudgingly – stepped up to the plate to help me polish up the story. You guys and gals mean the world to me and I'm thankful you're on my team: Jason, Louise, Aria, Diane, Caryl, Carol, and Elizabeth. I appreciate everything you do for me.

Handling the fantastic cover illustration was none other than, you guessed it, Felipe de Barros. As always, he's proven he's one talented artist and very thankful he knows what he's doing. Fantastic work as always, my friend!

Once more, I find myself needing to thank the one person who keeps me inspired and writing more adventures for Zack and the dogs: you! Thank you so much for purchasing this book and helping to support an indie author! I should also mention that the otter chapter graphic I used was created by Papapishu, and found at https://www.1001freedownloads.com/free-clipart/otter. Now, I don't really know who this person is, but I feel obligated to throw a shoutout in their direction, seeing how this person was responsible for creating a wonderful drawing and allowing others to use it.

With all that said, it's time to see what everyone has been up to!
Happy reading! J.

To Giliane —

We celebrated one helluva milestone this year, namely our 20th anniversary! How did we celebrate? By going to Europe! May the next 20 be just as fun!

ONE

Okay, you win. I'll admit it. It's really beautiful here. I've always heard about Monterey, but have never stopped to look around. Had I known that it looked like this, then it wouldn't have taken me quite as long to visit."

"I'm glad you think so, Zachary. I've always enjoyed coming down here to unwind. And, for the two of us, this was the perfect time to do it."

"Very true," I admitted.

I looked over at my companion, Ms. Jillian Cooper, and smiled at her. My girlfriend. I never thought that anyone would ever hold that particular title again, nor would I be so willing to jump back into a relationship. But, much to my surprise, not only was I willing, I felt incredibly happy to do so.

I guess I should explain.

My name is Zack Anderson. I was born and raised in Phoenix, Arizona, and lived there for the vast majority of my life. I married my high school sweetheart less than a month after graduating, and the two of us couldn't have been happier.

However, I received a brutal reality check one fateful day two years ago when my darling wife, Samantha, was taken from me much too early. You see, her car had collided head on with an oncoming semi-truck. Death was instantaneous.

My late wife's death had never sat well with me, and when I started receiving not-so-subtle hints that, perhaps, her death hadn't been an accident, well, I decided to return to my home state to do some investigating. But, that's another story.

The one thing I will say, though, is I really do appreciate my circle of friends. High on that list is Vance Samuelson, a detective living in the same small town as I do now, namely Pomme Valley, Oregon. He ended up accompanying me to Phoenix to see if we could figure out if there was more to Samantha's death than I was originally led to believe. Vance is married to a highly intelligent woman by the name of Tori. She's tall, lithe, has red hair, and teaches at the local high school. Also on that list was my best friend from high school, Harry Watt. I never would have imagined we'd both end up in the same small town, especially in the Pacific Northwest, of all places. However, Harry had put his partying days behind him, married a woman named Julie, had two kids, and became the town veterinarian. Harry was also the reason I was the owner of two dogs.

Sherlock and Watson. What can I say about those two? Well, let's start with the fact that they are corgis. Now, if you're familiar with the breed, you'll know there are two types of corgis. The easiest way to describe the difference is that, typically, the Pembrokes don't have any tails, whereas the Cardigans do. My two were both Pembrokes, and quite frankly, two of the smartest dogs I had ever seen. Sherlock and Watson were quite adept at catching criminals.

I kid you not.

Those two corgis have solved a number of crimes, including more murder cases than anyone in the entire Pomme Valley police department. It's a sore subject with the PV cops, but thankfully, they don't let it show. In fact, Chief Nelson hired me and the dogs as genuine police consultants a while back. This, coming from the one person who was convinced I was guilty of murder back when I first moved here.

But, that's another story, and it's one I've already told. As you can see, I've got quite a long and colorful past in PV. In that particular murder case, Sherlock was the main reason I was exonerated. He somehow managed to find the clues which proved my innocence. And ... the two of them have been doing the same ever since.

Fast forward to the present day. I was holding down three job titles, while Jillian ... I'm sorry. I guess I should explain the other two roles I hold in Pomme Valley. First and foremost, I am a romance author. I started writing while I was living in Phoenix, but not under my name, no. Behind the computer, I'm Chastity Wadsworth, risqué writer extraordinaire. Don't laugh. That name sells lots of books.

I'm also the owner of a highly profitable winery: Lentari Cellars. It is a local PV favorite, and after I inherited the winery and decided to reopen, I made a lot of friends. Who would've known disgusting, fermented grape juice could be so popular and worth so much? And yes, if you couldn't tell, I don't touch wine. Ever. It's not for any moral objections, I can assure you. Quite frankly, I wish I liked the stuff. My problem is my taste buds. I can't stand the taste of alcohol. If Caden, my wine master, had his way, then he'd have me drinking a bottle of wine every night until I started to enjoy it. Thus far, however, his attempts at turning me into a sommelier have failed. Miserably.

But, I really can't complain. The entire town loves my wine, er, Caden's wine, so much that there's around a three-month-long waiting list just to procure a bottle. And, since Caden is always looking to the future, he's talked me into expanding the winery's offerings. How? We're going to make some wine from fruit other than grapes. We now have apple trees, cherry trees, berry bushes, and so on. But, do you know what that means? I'm back to being Guinea Pig #1. I've had to sample all kinds of crap. That's why I have mini fridges stashed everywhere, crammed full of soda. I never know when Caden will come strolling up to me with his latest poison. Er, concoction. That also explains why I can look out my bedroom window and see the framework being erected on our new warehouse. Apparently, fruit wine takes a while to age. We'll need a place to store it.

All right. I think we have the bases covered. Romance writer? Check. Winery owner? Check. Police consultant with my two dogs? Check.

As for my girlfriend, Jillian is the owner of a local specialty kitchen store. Cookbook Nook focuses on cookbooks, kitchen gadgets, and has a small café on the second floor which serves a variety of local goodies. Jillian keeps the place organized, clean, and running efficiently, which means her store turns a tidy profit, too.

She's also part owner of quite a number of other local businesses; only she keeps that to herself. Jillian, like myself, is widowed. Her late husband, Michael, was quite the shrewd businessman and made certain that, should anything ever happen to him, Jillian wouldn't have to work again. Well, unfortunately for him, Michael contracted cancer and passed away. Jillian, after confiding to me that she was essentially the richest woman on the west coast, helped her friends realize their dreams by opening multiple businesses as their silent partner.

In fact, Jillian recently purchased one of PV's historic properties, Highland House. The house has quite a history behind it, including rumors of it being haunted. Well, we never found a ghost hiding within its walls. However, we did find all kinds of things there: hidden rooms, passageways, missing jewelry, and so on. Putting all that aside, though, I can tell you that house is going to make a fantastic bed and breakfast. I even met the lady Jillian had hired to run it, Lisa Martinez. Together, the two of them have the house looking spectacular and on track for its fall opening.

That explains why we're here. You can see what the two of us have been dealing with. We needed a break, and it was Jillian who came up with the winning plan, a road trip vacation. With the dogs, of course.

But, where to? Well, as you now know, we chose Monterey, California. I've never been here, but Jillian has on a number of occasions. Beautiful weather, gorgeous scenery, abundant wildlife, and a world-class aquarium, all within a town of less than 30,000 people. It was a perfect choice for the two of us to relax.

As was usual whenever it came to me, I was wrong. You'll see just how wrong I was this particular time in a little bit.

Now, let's get back to the two of us, well, make that the four of us. Jillian and I were strolling, hand in hand, along sandy McAbee Beach. I had always thought beaches like this weren't to be found in California. I mean, come on. I've seen the coastline in the northern part of the state. It's usually littered with huge, inhospitable rocks with not a grain of sand to be found anywhere. This, however, was a pleasant surprise. As for the dogs? Well, they were loving it.

Right on cue, I heard an excited yip. Sherlock, it would seem, was barking at the lapping waves. Every time the feisty corgi thought the water was venturing too close, he'd bark at it. And, as if the water had heard and was shying away, the waves would retreat. I also noticed the tri-colored corgi didn't mind getting his paws wet. Jillian and I would laugh so hard at his antics that Sherlock had even looked our way a few times to make sure we were okay. I mean, what else were we supposed to do when, as the waves retreated and Sherlock gave chase, the waves would come back and we'd have one corgi hauling butt to get back to the safety of dry land? Watson, on the other hand, was perfectly content to stay dry and avoided coming close to the water's edge. Oh, don't get me wrong, she'd add her two cents whenever Sherlock would, but she'd do it by the safety of her daddy's side, thank you very much.

Dogs.

As for me, I was on a quest. Kinda. Jillian had mentioned that a friend of hers had started making jewelry from bits of something called sea glass. I later learned it was just pieces of broken glass that had been tossed and tumbled by the water long enough to sand it smooth. Of the dozen or so pieces that I had found, nearly three-quarters had been rejected. They just weren't the right size and shape.

A piece of dark red glass caught my eye. I

stooped to retrieve it and then held it up to my eyes for inspection. I have no idea what shape the glass originally held, as I don't see many pieces of red glass anything, but this was too good a color to pass up. I triumphantly turned to Jillian and presented my find.

"Oooo, it's maroon! Where did you find this one?"

I pointed at the ground, "Right there. I'd love to know what this used to be a part of, but that's something we'll never know."

"This will work beautifully. Thank you."

"Did you find another one?" a male voice asked. Actually, it came off as more of a whine, if you ask me. "I don't know how you keep finding 'em, man."

I guess I should mention that we weren't alone on this trip. After learning the two of us were headed south for some much needed R & R with our dogs, our good friends, Harry and Julie, asked if they could tag along. Ordinarily, I would have objected, seeing how this could really mess up the plans that I had, but after Jillian confided to me that the two of them were hoping to rekindle the romance in their marriage, I relented. From what I've been told, and what I've observed over the last year or so, Harry and Julie have been at each other's throats more often than not. Thankfully, neither one of them enjoyed acting like that, especially to each other, so they thought a vacation away from their kids, focused only on them, was just what the doctor ordered.

"I did," I confirmed, as I looked back at my friend. Harrison Watt was a smidge taller than me, had a neatly trimmed full beard and, I'm sorry to say, nearly fifty pounds on me. "Jillian doesn't have this color. I don't know what she plans on doing with it yet, but I can't wait to see."

"I don't get it. I haven't found anything yet," my friend complained.

I pointed off to the side of where I was standing, "Would you like to know why?"

Harry jammed his hands into his pockets and frowned. "Hit me with your best shot."

"You're following behind me."

"So?"

"Harry, think about it. If you're following behind me, and I've already checked the area for any bits of sea glass, what are the odds you're going to find some?"

"Are you telling me you're hogging all the glass? Not cool, bro."

"That's why I'm telling you now," I said, swallowing my anger. "I'll check here, you check over there. In fact, look by your left foot. That's a nice piece of green glass."

"Hmm? What glass? I don't see any."

I squatted next to Harry's leg and gingerly picked up the piece of glass. I could tell from the rough shape that it probably came from one of the old Perrier mineral water bottles. This one had been in the water for so long that its edges were worn smooth and it bore a clouded film of scratches on it, which lightened the color considerably.

"You do know what you're looking for, don't you? Here. Hold this. Do you see the glass? It's a piece of a broken bottle, but the water has sanded it completely smooth and then buffed the front of it."

"What do you know," Harry muttered, as he studied the glass. "I was looking for clear glass, or something that looked like broken glass. So, that means this right here ... is this a piece?"

Harry held out a small dime-sized piece of sea glass. I nodded my head.

"Nice job. You found yourself a piece of sea glass."

"Jules, look! I found some!"

"Nice job!" Julie returned. "We've been at it for over thirty minutes and you just now found one piece?"

"He didn't know what he was looking for," I heard Jillian quietly explain. "You can't fault him for not finding anything just yet."

"Well, at least someone ... oof! Dude, what the he—?" Harry complained, as he rubbed his stomach. I had delivered a swift blow to his midsection.

"I think I see some more up ahead," I told Harry. I turned to Jillian. "We won't wander too far."

Sensing I wanted to talk to Harry, Jillian nodded. "We'll be right here."

As the two women began to talk in whispered

tones, I pulled a very reluctant Harry along with me as I put some distance between us and the girls.

"What'd you sucker punch me for, man? That wasn't nice."

"The last thing a woman wants to hear is a derogatory comment made to her in the presence of friends," I carefully and quietly explained. "Sure, you can have your arguments with her, but don't ridicule her. It'll never end well."

"Well, she needed to hear it," Harry grumped.

"Then let her hear it when the two of you are alone," I suggested. "You can be angry with her, but you still have to respect her. Try it. It'll work wonders, buddy. Trust me."

"Yeah, well ... maybe."

We walked on in silence for another few minutes. Behind us, I could hear the girls whispering between themselves. Concern for my friend had me pulling him to a stop.

"Are things okay with you and Julie?"

"Not really, man," Harry answered, with a sigh. "She always wants to go out and do something. I put in long hours at the clinic. All I want to do when I get home is put my feet up and have a few beers. Is that too much to ask for?"

"You don't think Julie works just as hard as you?" I countered. "You guys both need to unwind. Your kids are old enough to take care of themselves for a few hours, aren't they?"

Harry nodded. "Yeah. What's your point?"

"Do this. Next Friday, after the two of you get

home after work, suggest to Julie that you want to take her to dinner. Pick a nice restaurant. Get dressed up a bit."

"You didn't hear me, bro," Harry complained again. "I want to put my feet up after I get home."

"And the compromise," I slowly began, as I tried valiantly to refrain from throttling my dim-witted friend, "would be to look at it like this: for four days a week, you get to do just that. But, if you get into the habit of going out once, just the two of you, you'll find that Julie will be much more tolerant of you wanting to stay home during the week."

Harry shrugged. "I suppose I could do that."

"Then, on the weekend, take her out."

"But, I just did that! I mean, on Friday night, remember? Why do we have to go out again? That gets expensive, man."

"You don't have to buy something every time you go out," I explained.

"Huh? You don't?"

"No, you dillhole. Look, let's say you wake up Saturday, approach Julie, and suggest you go to the home improvement store. What do you think Julie would do?"

"She'd start planning the next project she'd want me to do, man. That's a terrible idea."

"No, it isn't," I insisted. "Listen, take her to the store and just look around. Get some ideas. You don't need to make any decisions right then and there. Let's say you have a light fixture that you need to replace ..."

"... which we do," Harry admitted. "Several."

"Right. Okay, let her pick out the fixture. Those aren't that expensive. They're easy to install, and ..."

"No way!" Harry practically cried. "You're talking 'bout messing with electricity. I'm not sticking my hands in an electrical panel, thank you very much. It's not my area of expertise. I'd be scared to death of getting zapped."

"Fine. Let her pick out the new light fixture ..."

"But ..."

"Let me finish. Let her pick it out and then give me a call. I'll help you install it."

"You know how to install something like that?"

"Piece of cake," I assured him. "I'll show you how to do it."

"I s'pose," Harry mumbled.

"See? It's things like that. Show her that you still care about her. Umm, you do, don't you?"

"What? Of course I do."

"Then you need to start acting like it. If you lose her, then you'll have no one to blame but yourself."

"I hear you, man. Thanks."

"Thanks? For what?"

"Thanks for the advice."

I looked back at Jillian and nodded. The smile she gave me could have lit up the entire night sky. Er, if it happened to be dark, that is. Harry and I waited for the girls to catch up and then we separated back into the appropriate couples.

"How'd that go?" Jillian quietly asked.

"Pretty good," I said. "He says he just wants to come home and put his feet up, even though Julie is always suggesting they go out. I gave him a compromise."

"And that is?" Jillian prompted.

"Start up a date night. Take her to dinner. Then, on the weekend, take her out somewhere. He doesn't have to buy her anything. It's the thought that counts."

"It's getting out of the house that counts," Jillian corrected.

Just then, Harry and Julie caught up to us. I looked expectantly back at Harry, who simply shrugged. Concerned, I looked over at Julie, who gave me a small smile.

"Tell us how things are going with Highland House," Julie began. "How close are you to finishing up with the renovations?"

"Within the next two weeks," Jillian answered. "The furniture has been cleaned, reupholstered, and repaired as needed. It's already starting to be returned to the house. I've even begun to pull things out of storage, to return them to the house."

"And, the, er, jewelry?" Julie hesitantly asked. "Are you sure you found it all?"

Jillian shrugged. "I may never know. I'm fairly confident that we've found what we could."

"What about that great big jewel?" Harry

asked, suddenly interested. "What did you do with that thing, anyway? Didn't you tell us it was worth nearly nine figures?"

"Nowhere near that much," Jillian laughed.

I kept my mouth shut. That was almost true. The *Czarina's Tear* had been appraised for nearly 75 million, but that didn't need to be common knowledge.

"The *Tear* is on loan to a museum in Chicago," Jillian answered. "They claim to have a security system which rivals Fort Knox, so I know the gem is protected."

"Some people get all the luck," Harry angrily grumbled.

I noticed a look of surprise, and then anger, appear on Julie's face. Still holding Jillian's hand, I gave it a warning squeeze and then gave a slightly perceptible nod of my head in Harry's direction. Jillian was careful to face forward as she rolled her eyes.

"I wouldn't worry about that jewel," Jillian began. "I prefer to keep it some place other than my home. The last thing I want people to know is that a gemstone worth eight figures is in my house. So, let the museum keep it."

"You're letting the museum *keep* it?" Harry all but squeaked, with surprise.

"That's not what I meant," Jillian hastily said.

"We're letting it be studied, admired, and so on," I said, coming to Jillian's aid. "What about you? I hear you're thinking about adding another doctor to your staff?"

"I don't know, man," Harry said. "They're expensive. All the ones I've talked to want a heckuva lot of money."

I heard a soft groan from Julie and realized I needed to change the subject. Rapidly.

"Hey, listen. We've broken ground on the new warehouse for Lentari Cellars. We need to clear out some inventory. I've got five extra cases of Syrah lying around. Four of the cases would make those on the waiting list happy. As for the fifth, well, would you guys like it?"

"A whole case?" Harry exclaimed, his gloomy mood evaporating faster than a fog bank in the full sun. "Are you serious, bro?"

I nodded. "There could be more. Caden and I are going through what storerooms we have, trying to take stock of everything. The next harvest will be bottled soon. We're going to need all the room we can get."

"We'd be delighted," Julie told us. "Thank you, Zachary."

"Yeah," Harry echoed. "Thanks, bro!"

"Thank you," Jillian mouthed.

I nodded and then shrugged. While none of that story had been true, the loss of a simple case of wine was a more than acceptable price to pay in order to get our two friends to stop bickering.

Just then, I felt the leashes I had been holding go taut. I automatically glanced over at the dogs. Sherlock and Watson were both at the water's edge, staring out at the open ocean. Curious as to what had caught their attention, I arrived at their side. Jillian followed moments later.

"What is it?" Jillian asked.

I shrugged. "I'm not sure. I don't see ... wait. Hmm, I *do* see something. Do you see it? About 100 feet that way, to the west. There's something floating in the water. At least, I think there is."

Sunset was less than an hour away, so that meant the four of us were practically staring straight at the sun, and shading our eyes with our hands. It made it hard to see, but there was definitely something floating on the water. Something black.

"I think ..." I began, as I studied the strange object, "it might be a sea lion. I've seen a few in the area."

"I don't think that's a sea lion," Julie told me, as she squinted at the distant object. "It looks like ... oh, dear lord. It looks like someone floating on the water, only they're face down!"

Jillian covered her mouth in horror. Within seconds, Julie was doing the same. As for Harry, well, he grunted once and shook his head in bewilderment. Wasn't someone going to do something? I mean, what if it was a person? Wouldn't they need some help? And, obviously if they're floating face down in the water, then they did. That meant one of us was going to have to swim out there to pull them in. I certainly didn't expect either of the girls to do it. That left me and Harry.

You may remember me mentioning Harry had —conservatively—at least fifty pounds on me? He was nowhere close to being in shape. In fact, he'd probably have a heart attack if he tried any amount of physical activity. Seriously, I was going to have to see about getting him to lay off the beers. It couldn't possibly be healthy for him. All that aside, though, it meant it was up to Yours Truly to swim all the way out there to see if the person needed help.

"Aww, maaann."

I quickly passed the leashes to Julie while tossing my cell and wallet to Jillian. I was about ready to head into the water when I remembered something. Experts always said that, if you had to jump in the water with your clothes on, then at the very least, remove your shoes. Why? That was because wearing shoes would make your feet feel heavier, and therefore make you swim in a disorderly manner.

"Shoes, Zachary," Jillian reminded me, as if she had been reading my mind.

"Yeppers. I'm on it."

"Be careful," Julie added.

Kicking off my shoes, I waded into the water and within seconds, sucked in a breath. Holy moly! This water was freezing! Hours later, when Jillian and I were recovering in our hotel room, I found out why. The temperature of the water all along the northern Californian coast was typically a balmy 55°F. Now, that may not sound too bad, but trust me. It was cold. I wasn't going to be able to last long in it.

The ground dropped off and I was forced to begin swimming. Keeping my eyes fixated on the black form ahead of me, I steadily swam toward what I was fervently hoping was something other than a dead human being. I mean, if it was a dead body, that meant I was gonna have to try and drag it back to shore.

"Don't be a corpse, don't be a corpse, don't be a corpse," I chanted to myself, as I labored to keep my arms and feet moving. The last thing I wanted to know was that I was in the water with a dead person at the same time.

Sure enough, Julie had called it. It was a body, and it was floating, face down, in the water. But why was it black, you ask? Well, that's because the body was wearing a neoprene wet suit.

Oh, joy. We had just found a dead scuba diver.

TWO

Which one of you was the one who found him?" a gruff voice asked, nearly thirty minutes later.

I raised a hand and ordered myself again to stop shivering. "Th-that w-would be me."

"Really," Jillian scolded. "Do we have to do this right this second? Zachary is freezing. That water is ice cold. Can we do this later, when he has had a chance to warm up?"

"It's all r-right," I said to Jillian, as I held her hand. "I'll b-be okay. Ask away, p-pal."

The four of us were sitting on some large, nearby boulders. I had a bright orange emergency blanket draped around my shoulders, and two uniformed medics were just finishing up a routine medical checkup on me. I guess everything was fine, because they began putting things back in their kits and then promptly left afterward.

I looked up at the two cops, who had been watching, and tried grinning, only my teeth wouldn't stop chattering. Trust me, it made trying to talk interesting. The first cop, the one who had asked who found the body, stepped forward. He was tall, in his mid-fifties, and had thinning gray hair. He was holding a clipboard and looked annoyed, as though he was angry with me for making him do some paperwork. There was also a young female cop with him, who thus far, hadn't said anything. She was probably in her late twenties, had bright red hair pulled up into a tight bun, and seemed uncertain about what she had to do. Perhaps she was a rookie?

"For the record, only one of you went in?" the senior cop asked, as he looked at the four of us.

"Yes," Julie answered. "We all spotted the body, but Zack was the one who volunteered to go out there to offer help."

"Do you have any idea who it is, man?" Harry asked.

"Divers don't typically carry ID in their wetsuits," the female cop said, speaking her first words. "I'm a diver myself. I never carry ID on a dive. It's usually stored in a locker, or with a friend who stays on the beach."

A question popped into my brain, but I wanted to wait a few moments. I was hopeful that I was done shivering for the time being.

"H-have you found any vehicles n-nearby?" Darn it. Why couldn't I warm up? I must sound like a stuttering idiot. "Wh-what about the other diver?"

"What other diver?" the first cop asked, interested. "Did you see another diver?"

I shook my head. "Well, n-no, but that goes against everything you're t-taught when you learn to dive."

"And what's that?" the older cop wanted to know.

"Never dive alone," the female cop answered, giving me a nod of appreciation.

"And how would you know that?" the second cop suspiciously asked, as he turned to look my way.

"He learned to dive in high school," Harry answered for me. "I know it might come as a shock, but we both did. Our P.E. instructor was one sadistic son of a—"

Julie smacked him on the arm.

"Watch your mouth."

Harry shrugged. "Whatever. Zack's right. You don't dive alone, bro. Too many bad things can happen."

"Like this," Jillian softly said.

"I wonder what he died of," I mused, more to myself than to anyone.

The female cop shrugged. "He probably just ... Oh, cute dogs. Are they yours?"

I looked over at Sherlock and Watson. Their ears were up, they were unblinking, and they were staring straight at the officers. If I didn't know any better, then I'd say that neither dog trusted the two strangers. Why the corgis were giving the cops the stink eye, I wasn't sure.

Giving a grunt of exasperation, the older cop

moved off, heading in the direction where the M.E. was standing. The female cop squatted next to the dogs and held out her hand. Both dogs gave it a cautious sniff before each gave the hand a single lick. Grinning, the woman stood and held out a hand, the same which had just been licked.

"Officer Marianne Adolphson."

I shook the offered hand. "Z-Zack Anderson. This is Jillian Cooper."

Harry then held out his hand and made his and Julie's introductions. Remembering the dogs, I took a breath and was about to say their names when Sherlock decided I wasn't moving fast enough for his liking and let out a short, ear-splitting bark. I ruffled the fur behind his ears and looked up at the cop.

"And this is Sherlock. He doesn't like to be excluded from introductions. Sniffing your right foot is Watson."

"Sherlock and Watson? Wait. Tell me you're not from Oregon. What was the name of that town ... Pomme Valley?"

I shook my head as Jillian let out a delighted laugh.

"Unreal. You've heard of my dogs?"

"Are these really the two dogs I've heard so much about?" Officer Adolphson asked, as she pulled out her cell. She promptly snapped a few pics and then, presumably, sent them off to a few of her contacts.

"They're really them," I admitted. "Tell me

something, Officer, how ..."

"Please," Officer Adolphson interrupted. "Call me Mary. It's easier."

"Thanks. Okay, Mary, how do you know my two dogs?"

"Are you kidding?" she exclaimed. "Everyone knows all about them. These two have solved two murder cases and located some type of valuable missing pendant. News like that will make the rounds, I assure you."

"Two murders?" Harry repeated, frowning. "It's more than that, isn't it?"

"They are up to, er, seven or eight murders now," I corrected, "and that doesn't include busting a dognapping organization and locating a ton of jewelry missing since the 1940s."

Mary stared at the dogs with wonder in her eyes.

"Oh, and don't forget earlier this year," Jillian said. "They solved your late wife's murder case in Phoenix."

I snapped my fingers. "Forgot about that one. Seriously, I'm losing track of all of the cases they've closed. I honestly don't know how they do it. I'm just here to make sure they get their kibble twice a day."

The older cop suddenly appeared by Mary's side.

"If you're done socializing, Officer Adolphson," the senior cop said, with a little bit of a sneer in his voice, "perhaps you could help me look for any signs of this mysterious second diver?"

"Of course, Officer Lewis. Umm, I feel I should tell you something."

"Oh?"

"Do you see the two dogs there?"

"Of course. What about them? This is public land. As long as the owners clean up after them, they're allowed to be here."

Mary nodded. "Correct. However, I was referring to their names. They are Sherlock and Watson, from Oregon. You heard about them. We were just talking about them last week."

One bushy gray eyebrow was raised, in true Vulcan fashion.

"Is that so? These two are the crime fighting canines from Pomme Valley?"

"Guilty as charged," I admitted.

"And I am to believe that these two dogs have solved a murder case?"

"More than that, I'm afraid," I corrected. "I forget the number of cases, but the number of murders is somewhere around eight."

"You forgot Samantha's case again," Harry reminded me. "She wasn't in PV, man, but she still counts."

"Right. I guess that'd be nine."

"They've solved nine murders?" Officer Lewis repeated, incredulous. "Impossible."

I shrugged. "Believe it. Don't believe it. It doesn't matter. As for that poor diver? I'm guessing it was just an accident. Maybe he ran out of air, maybe he became tired, or ..."

"... a current could have pulled him under," Mary suggested, after I trailed off.

"What are you doing here?" Officer Lewis asked me, after he gave Mary a scowl.

"Just taking a vacation with some friends," I answered. "We're not here to cause any trouble. This is my first visit, and my girlfriend wanted to show me around. Harry and Julie over there are close friends who are traveling with us."

"How long will you be in town?" Officer Lewis wanted to know.

"A few days. Why?"

"Don't go ..." Officer Lewis trailed off as a phone began to ring. Fishing his cell from his pocket, he grunted once, and turned away, walking in the opposite direction.

"Don't mind him," Mary told us. "He was supposed to be fishing right now, and seeing how we're short-handed, he had his PTO canceled."

"That isn't our fault, man," Harry said, frowning.

"I think he's talking to the captain," Mary said, as she turned to look back at the direction Lewis had wandered off. "I'll go check on him. Will you guys be staying in this area for a little bit?"

Jillian nodded. "We will be, yes."

At the exact same time Mary walked away, I watched Jillian suddenly turn to look at the dogs. She was still holding their leashes, and at the moment, both Sherlock and Watson were looking northwest. Curious to see what they were looking at, I rose up on my tip-toes to see over the ridge and out at the water. The problem was, that's all there was in that direction: water. Stretching endlessly away to the west, all I could see was the gentle lapping of the waves as they crashed into the rocks, which then had the water working its way up as high as it could onto the shore.

"They want to go that way," Jillian told me. "Should I let them?"

I was now dry enough to put my shoes back on, so I nodded and waved her on.

"Go ahead. I'll catch up."

Five minutes later, I crested the small ridge and was approaching a bend on the shore. I could clearly hear Jillian and Julie talking together in the distance, as well as see the footprints in the sand, which led in the same direction I was headed. But, as I approached the water's edge, I could see that they were still a decent distance ahead of me. Both dogs were sniffing along the ground and guiding the three of them farther north along the shore. Then, as one, they stopped and turned their heads to look back at me. By the time I caught up, the two ladies were laughing about something, and Harry was sulking. Hopefully, it wasn't something at his expense, but seeing how Jillian would never shame someone, even if she had reason to, I figured one of the girls must have told a funny story. Hmm. Now that I thought about it, if the funny story was about me, then Jillian would be sharing it with everyone.

"What's the matter?" I whispered, as I approached my friend's side.

"I just wish I knew what they were laughing at, man," Harry quietly grumbled.

"You think they're laughing about you?" I softly asked.

"What do you think?" Harry sourly asked. "Of course they are."

I angrily grabbed Harry's arm and pulled him off to the side and out of earshot from the girls.

"Look, pal. I don't know what's bugging you. I don't know why you're acting so depressed. You've got a wife who absolutely loves you. You've got two adorable kids, a fantastic house, and a successful business. I should also mention you have immaculate taste in friends. You have got absolutely nothing to be angry over." I turned to look at the two women and hooked a thumb in their direction. "And those two? I hereby wager that, if they're laughing at one of us, it isn't you, but me."

"There's no way," Harry insisted. "Julie likes to make fun of me."

"If she does, then you need to learn to laugh at yourself," I advised him. "No one likes being ridiculed, but people love to laugh at those who can take a joke. I can't begin to tell you how many times I've been laughed at. But, back to the girls. You think they're laughing at you? Bet me. I say I'm the one they're laughing at."

"Fine. What do you want to bet?"

"Hmm. If I'm right, and I win, then I want you to make a conscious effort to relax. This is a vacation. Have fun."

"I guess I can do that."

"You didn't let me finish."

Harry sighed. "I knew that was too easy. Fine. What else do you want me to do?"

"At dinner tonight, you will eat whatever I order for you."

"Dude. You drive a hard bargain. Fine. And if I win?"

I shrugged. "I don't know. What do you want me to do?"

"Something as heinous as what you'll put me through tonight, that's for sure."

I grinned. "I'm waiting, amigo. You must have something in mind. And, I should tell you, all culinary wagers are off the table."

"You're no fun."

"Frog legs. I ate frog legs, Harry. Let's see you top that."

"That was pretty wicked," Harry admitted. A smile finally formed on my friend's face. "I've got it, bro. If I win, then you will volunteer at the clinic. I have some kennels that need to be scrubbed out."

My eyebrows shot up. Me? Cleaning dirty dog kennels? Why, that sneaky, two-timing ... okay, fair's fair.

"You're on. Hey, Jillian?"

My girlfriend's head turned and she gave me a beaming smile, "Yes?"

"Just now, what were you and Julie laughing about?"

"Oh, uh, it was nothing."

"I need to settle a bet," I said, as I gave Harry a sideways glance. "There's a lot riding on this."

"I don't think you want to know, Zachary," Jillian giggled.

Oh, man. The nagging little voice in my head suddenly decided that, even if I did win the bet, I was still going to end up losing. Maybe this wasn't a smart idea after all?

"You can tell me," I groaned. "I can take it."

I hope.

"Well, all right. Just remember, you asked for it."

"Perhaps I should have just asked if you were telling a story about me," I mumbled.

Jillian nodded. "That would have been the smart thing to do. The answer? Yes, of course."

I triumphantly turned to Harry. "See? I told you they were talking about me. Hah! Now, I expect you to honor the wager. And I know you know what that means. Besides, we're gonna have some fun tonight, aren't we?"

"Yeah, yeah. Swell. Hey, wait! What was the story? What was so funny?"

"That's really not necessary," I hastily interjected. "It doesn't need to be told."

"It does if you think I'm gonna let you pick out

my entree tonight," Harry argued.

Julie stared at her husband in amazement, "You're going to let him pick out your choice of dinner tonight? Dare I ask what he would have had to do should he have lost?"

"Kennel cleaning," Harry chuckled. "Okay, Jillian. Spill. What's the story?"

Jillian helplessly looked over at me and gave me an apologetic smile. "Well, this was a story Zachary told me when we were comparing embarrassing stories one night last week. This happened before I met him. It happened on a road trip from Phoenix to Los Angeles, where Zack stopped at a roadside rest area."

I felt all the color drain from my face. I suddenly knew what story Jillian had been sharing, and the thought had me cringing. Of all the infernal luck, she had to tell that one?

"Zachary was wearing a t-shirt and cargo shorts," Jillian explained, looking at Harry. "The kind with large pockets in the front. Do you know the kind I mean?"

Harry nodded. "I have several pair. Why is that funny?"

Jillian's eyes sparkled with amusement as she noticed the embarrassed look on my face, "Well, the problem came with his belt."

"His belt?" Harry repeated, confused. "I don't get it."

"You will," Julie snickered, as she looked my way and giggled.

Jillian suddenly pointed at my belt, "Do you see what's on Zack's belt right now? I'm talking about that black pouch by his right hip."

"Yeah, I see it. What about it?"

"It's his multi-tool gadget," Jillian explained. "He always carries it with him."

"Okay. So?"

I groaned, drawing Harry's eyes to my own.

"What am I missing?"

"It's heavy, Harry," I sighed. "If you're standing in front of a urinal, and you unbuckle your belt, especially for the first time since strapping that thing to your belt, then what's going to happen when you let go of the belt to, ah, take care of business?"

Harry's eyes widened and he started to snicker.

"That's right," I nodded. "My shorts fell to the floor so fast it was as though someone had come up behind me and yanked them down. Needless to say, it was a busy day, and the place was packed."

Harry let out a loud guffaw and grinned at me. He finally nodded.

"Okay, man. You win. Just go easy on me."

I smiled back at my friend. "Like hell I will. You had better plan on bringing some Tums tonight."

Then we heard a series of loud, high-pitched yips. Sherlock and Watson were both pulling on their leashes, anxious to resume moving. I thought I had heard most of the noises the corgis were capable of producing, but the yips both dogs were making now was a new one on me. Was it excitement? Frustration? A combination of both?

Jillian passed me Sherlock's leash as I took the lead. Winding our way down a well-used path, we traveled another three hundred feet north before coming to a sudden stop. Sherlock yipped once and fell silent. About ready to squat down to see if there was anything wrong with him, such as a thorn in his paw, or perhaps check to be sure his harness wasn't too tight, I heard an answering sound.

Just then, a series of chirps, almost bird-like in nature, echoed back at us. Both of the corgis' ears jumped straight up, and both, I might add, resumed pulling on their leashes, eager to get to ... the water. I peered anxiously in that direction, eager to see what was at the water, waiting for them. What I saw drew me up short.

It was a small group of sea otters, floating together in the water. I remember reading from somewhere that otters tended to hang out together for safety reasons, and that they had a very high metabolism. That meant they spent the majority of their day eating, and when they weren't eating, then they were primping their fur. Otters had the densest coats of fur on any animal, having nearly a million hairs per square inch. They didn't rely on fat, but their coats, to keep them warm, so at any given moment you could find an otter cleaning its fur.

This particular group numbered around two dozen and all of them, I might add, were staring straight at us. Nearly three-quarters of their numbers were eating, whether it was mussels, crab, or some type of shellfish. Hooked together to keep from floating away, the otters continued to stare at us, as though they were trying to decide if we were dangerous or not.

Sherlock led me right up to the water's edge, which placed him nearly fifteen feet from the otters. Keeping a tight grip on his leash, I stood, motionless, as I stared at the cute, snuggly-looking bundles of fur staring back at us. Jillian appeared by my side moments later.

"Oh, they're so cute!"

"True, but they're still wildlife," I reminded her. "Look at the size of them. They're bigger than the dogs."

Jillian nodded. "Right. No petting. Harry, that goes for you, too."

"Why would you think I'd do something like that?" Harry asked.

I turned to my friend and regarded him in silence for a few moments.

"What?" PV's veterinarian demanded. "I didn't do anything."

"Now," I clarified. "However, you can't say that you didn't do anything like that in the past."

"When have I ever tried to touch wildlife?" Harry wanted to know. He looked at Julie and smiled sheepishly. "Honestly, I don't know where Zack comes up with this stuff, man. I would never ..."

"Oh, don't give me that," I interrupted. "Think back to senior year. Do you remember what we all did for the senior prank?"

Surprisingly, Harry shook his head. "No, I actually don't. Whatever it is you think I did, I didn't do it. I never …"

"Bear poop."

Harry stopped in mid-sentence. He stared at me for a few moments before a huge grin appeared on his face. A shit-eating grin, if you'll pardon the pun. He suddenly looked at Julie and sobered.

"Umm, it's all hearsay. Don't buy it, Jules."

"What did he do, Zachary?" Julie asked, ignoring Harry and turning to me. "What's this about bear poop?"

"It has to be some of the nastiest, smelliest, most disgusting poop known to exist. Strange, if you think about all the different animals that are out there, but you need to trust me on this one. The zoo in Phoenix had three polar bears. Every single night, the poop was collected and stored in white five-gallon buckets, which were placed just outside a certain gate."

Jillian wrinkled her nose. "Eww. Why would they do that?"

"The swing keeper would then come by not long afterward and collect the buckets, so that it could be disposed of properly."

Julie turned to her husband. "You stole a bucket."

"I did not!" Harry protested. He pointed at me.

"How come you're not accusing Zack? He's the one who stole it."

Julie crossed her arms over her chest, "He would never do something like that."

"That's true," I admitted, drawing a scowl from Harry. "Now. But, back then? Yeah, that was me. I stole the poo."

Jillian turned to me with a look of surprise written all over her face.

"Zachary, you didn't."

"We were young and really dumb," I said, by way of answer.

"What did you do with the bucket?" Julie asked.

I looked over at Harry and grinned. "Perhaps you'd like to take it from here, pal. You're the one who stole the bucket from me."

Harry fidgeted uncomfortably. "I, uh, may have left it inside the principal's office, with the lid removed."

"That's disgusting!" Julie exclaimed.

"It really was," I recalled. "But, I heard the lid was left next to the bucket, so that it could be sealed back up. I know, it was a stupid prank. But, in our defense, no one got hurt."

The chirping from the water suddenly quieted, which drew all of our attention. Sherlock was still at the water's edge and was standing, with his front left paw curled under him, as though he was trying to decide whether or not to take another step. What I saw next had me reaching for my phone. Not to call anyone, mind you, but to start recording what was transpiring in front of me.

One of the young otters had apparently awoken from its nap, spotted Sherlock nearby, and was slowly edging closer. The otter swam up to the water's edge, eyed Sherlock, and then cooed at him, just like a dove would. The tri-colored corgi still hadn't budged an inch. Sherlock watched the strange creature approach, and when it appeared as though the foreign *dog* wanted to sniff noses, he edged forward to do just that. The otter, on the other hand, wasn't too sure what Sherlock was doing, so it curiously leaned forward to get a better look.

Otter and corgi ended up touching noses.

Sherlock snorted once and then pawed at his nose, as though he had just dunked his snout in water. The corgi's actions had the effect of spurring the otter back to deeper water. Within moments, nearly a dozen of the larger adult otters were within reach. At first, I became worried for Sherlock's safety, and started to pull him back toward me. Then, I realized the otters weren't there to fight. They wanted to play!

Four of them ventured up to us and sat up on their haunches, as if they were trying to make a decision how to proceed. That's when I noticed Watson had appeared by Sherlock's side, which meant Jillian was now standing next to me. She had her phone in her hand, too, only I don't know if it was to take pictures or to call someone.

"Wild otters can be dangerous," Jillian said, by way of explanation.

I watched the otters, who were watching the dogs. They were chittering, chirping, and cooing as they raced up onto the beach, took a step or two out of the water, and then bolted back to the safety of the ocean. Sherlock, recognizing play, dropped his head and yipped.

The otters chirped back. This playful banter lasted a little over five minutes, until the otters determined it was time for another snack and drifted away from the shore. Nearly half disappeared beneath the waves but then reappeared not long afterward, clutching some type of food in their paws. We saw mussels; several were holding small crabs, but the vast majority of them had some type of shellfish.

Whackwhackwhackwhack.

"It's got a righteous beat to it, doesn't it?" Harry chuckled.

"They're breaking open the clams," I observed. "It looks like they're carrying around something hard with which to break the shells. That's what they're doing: smashing the shells open."

"Clever," Julie added.

The otter that had touched noses with Sherlock was floating on its back with the others and was holding a small black mussel in its paws, but it only had eyes for the dogs. It cooed a few times before it, too, began the rhythmic beating which signaled the beginning of its dinner. After a few moments, however, it suddenly dropped the shell it had been holding, bolted upright, and let out a noise that sounded a lot like the word *hah*, only loud and clipped.

Just like that, every single otter in the group discarded their meals and were floating upright in the water. I heard several hisses, and then the otters dove out of sight. Confused, I looked at my girlfriend.

"What just happened? What spooked them?"

Jillian pointed at the dogs. "Zachary, look! Whatever spooked the otters has spooked them, too!"

Sure enough, Sherlock's hackles were raised, and he was letting off several warning woofs. Watson scooted closer to Jillian's side and whined. A split second later, I slapped a hand over my nose.

"Dang, Watson. You haven't done that in a while. Whew. I'm glad we're outside."

For those who may not be familiar with my little girl, Watson has been known to be a little gassy at times. Don't get me wrong, she's much better than she has been. Right after I got her, the stench was so bad, and was happening so frequently, that I had to seek advice from Harry. He explained that some dogs fart because they take in air when they're eating. It can happen if the dog eats too fast. Well, Watson could empty her bowl in less than twenty seconds. And that, I'm sorry to say, caused her to inadvertently gulp air, and ... well, the air has to go somewhere.

"Dude, *what* are you feeding her?" Harry exclaimed, as he fanned the air. "I thought you told me she wasn't farting as much."

"She wasn't. Isn't. This is the first in a few months."

"Maybe the poor thing is scared," Jillian suggested, as she squatted low to put an arm around the red and white corgi.

I looked back at Sherlock and narrowed my eyes. He was staring straight at a row of waist-high shrubs. Was an otter hiding back there? Or, worse yet, was there something else hiding back there?

I handed Sherlock's leash back to Jillian and motioned for Harry to join me. For once, he didn't put up any arguments. Together, we carefully skirted around the bushes and, on the count of three, made a loud, whooping noise.

"Aaauuugh!!"

A wild-eyed, young woman popped up in the middle of the bushes and then smiled sheepishly when she realized the four of us were staring at her. She looked to be in her early twenties, had short, curly black hair, and was tall, around 5'10". She was wearing a dark green t-shirt, with some type of white logo on the upper left breast pocket, khaki shorts, and white shoes.

"Who are you?" I demanded. "Why were you hiding from us?"

"I wasn't!" the girl protested.

"You're standing in the middle of a bush," Jillian pointed out, using a neutral voice.

At this point, I caught Harry's eyes and nodded back in the direction we had come from. My friend nodded knowingly and hurried off.

"Who are you?" I asked. "Were you spying on us?"

"No!" the woman indignantly cried.

"Then explain yourself," I continued. "What were you doing here?"

Jillian suddenly took a step closer and stared hard at the woman's face.

"Excuse me, have you been crying?"

The woman automatically wiped her face with her hands.

"Of course not. Why would you say that?"

"Because you have," Julie said, as she joined Jillian. "Your eyes are swollen, your nose is red, and you have bags under your eyes. What ... the diver! You know about the diver, don't you?"

A fresh tear streaked down the woman's face before she could wipe it away with her hand.

"Did you know him?" Jillian gently asked.

The woman nodded and then started sobbing.

Jillian pulled a tissue from her purse and offered it to the woman.

"Who was he? Was he someone close to you?"

I caught Jillian and Julie's eyes and indicated we should head back toward the scene of the crime. Jillian nodded and held out a hand. The woman in the green shirt took it and carefully stepped out of the bush.

"This isn't what it looks like," the woman began.

I nodded. "I hope so, because it looks like you were relieving yourself in there."

Jillian smacked me on the arm. "Zachary! This woman's upset. Now's not the time for jokes."

"I thought it was funny," Julie quietly confided to me.

I grinned at her. "Thanks."

We arrived back at the crime scene and saw Harry had already made it back and was talking to the same two cops. Catching sight of us, he said something and then pointed at us. The senior cop glanced over, saw the woman walking with us, and his face became grim. He said something to Mary, which resulted in Officer Adolphson hurrying over to intercept us.

"Officer Marianne Adolphson," Mary announced, as we arrived. "Monterey Police Department. And who might you be?"

"Sh-Sherry. Sherry VanZanten."

"Is it true? Were you caught hiding in the bushes?"

"I wasn't hiding in the bushes," Sherry protested again. "I was simply collecting my thoughts. I heard a body had been discovered, and when I went to see for myself who it was, I saw that it was Jack. I clearly didn't handle the news well."

"Jack?" Mary repeated, as she pulled out a small notebook. "Jack who?"

"Jack Carlton. He's an aquarist for Monterey

Bay Aquarium."

"And how did you hear Mr. Carlton had passed away?" Mary asked, frowning. "His body was only discovered less than 30 minutes ago."

Sherry turned to point at a series of buildings a half mile away.

"I work right over there. Do you see those buildings? They're part of MBA. Whenever I have a break, I like to walk along the beach."

"Where the body of a deceased diver just happened to turn up," Officer Lewis' voice suddenly said, making us all jump. Sherlock woofed a warning at the unfriendly policeman.

"We work in the same department," Sherry told us. "Our paths are bound to cross, which they do, dozens of times each day. What's your point? Are you accusing me of something?"

"Take down Ms. VanZanten's statement," Officer Lewis said,

Mary nodded, and turned back to Sherry as the senior officer pulled out his cell and made a few calls. "What can you tell us about the deceased? Where does he live? What type of work does he do?"

"Who, Jack? Well, he has an apartment here, in Monterey, but he also kept apartments in New York City, London, and Wellington."

"Wellington?" Mary repeated, as she looked up.

"New Zealand," I answered.

Mary nodded. "Thanks. He has apartments all around the globe, huh? He must be paid very well."

"He was," Sherry confirmed, "but not just from MBA. He was an on-call diver for National Geographic. They sent him all over the world."

"To do what?" I asked.

"To dive, to capture underwater shots, to conduct census checks of certain species. You name it, he did it. And NGC had him doing practically everything."

"This guy sounded like he enjoyed his adventures," Jillian remarked.

"Jack may not have been at MBA full-time, but he had more volunteers than anyone. Everyone wanted a chance to work with him."

"What was he like?" Julie asked. "Did he get along with everybody? Could someone have done this to him?"

Sherry shook her head. "Oh, heavens no. Everyone loved him. He was, far and away, the most popular aquarist at MBA. They are going to be devastated by his loss."

"Someone that popular usually has people who are jealous of them," I commented.

Sherry shrugged. "Possibly, but not around here."

Harry suddenly raised a hand. "I have a question. Based on what you're telling us, would you say this Jack guy was an experienced diver?"

"One of the best in the world," Sherry confirmed.

"So, where was his diving partner?"

Sherry shrugged. "I really don't know. I can

only assume they were somehow separated. You'd have to look at his dive log to know for sure. He keeps meticulous records."

"And where would we find this dive log?" Mary wanted to know.

Sherry pointed at the buildings in the distance. "In his office, of course."

Officer Lewis finished his call and joined Mary. "What do you have? Anything to go on?"

"His name is Jack Carlton, and he's a world-famous diver and explorer," Mary answered. "And, we should probably check his diving log. Mr. Carlton wouldn't have gone scuba diving alone, and right now, we're missing a diver."

THREE

Monterey Bay is known for its spectacular diving locales, its picturesque beaches, and abundant wildlife. Also on that list is the historic Cannery Row, a waterfront street in the New Monterey section of town. Lining the street are defunct sardine canneries, with several of them now housing hotels and restaurants. The popularity of Cannery Row continues to grow each year, due to the availability of extensive public fishing amenities.

Seeing how we weren't invited to try and hunt down this missing diver, and after the local police department assured us that they had things well in hand, we took some time to explore Cannery Row the following day. The four of us.... Sorry, I keep doing that. With the dogs, there are six of us.

Okay. Let's try that again.

Today, the six of us are walking through Cannery Row, stopping at gift shops, attractions, and pretty much anything that catches our eye. Some of the stores allowed dogs. Others didn't. For those that didn't, I volunteered to wait outside while Jillian and Julie perused the wares. Harry, more often than not, elected to wait outside with me. We had just left one little boutique, which specialized in socks, of all things, when we stepped across a cross-street and came face to face with another shop. Jillian immediately came to a stop and I saw that her face had lit up.

It was a Thomas Kinkade gallery.

"Oooo, let's go inside. Do you think they allow dogs?"

"We most certainly do," the female clerk assured us as she held the door open.

Since the weather was a beautiful 72 degrees, the shop's front door was wide open and the female attendant was standing outside, hoping to entice customers to venture inside. The woman squatted next to the corgis and stroked the fur on the top of their heads.

"My, aren't you two some of the cutest dogs I've seen in a while? What are their names?"

"That's Sherlock," I answered, pointing at the corgi who was sniffing the attendant's pockets in the hopes she might be hiding a biscuit. "And that's Watson, on your left."

"Sherlock and Watson. That's adorable!"

"We think so," Jillian added, as she gave the woman a friendly smile.

"Wow, these things are pricey!" I heard Harry exclaim, as he stopped to read the price tag of the first painting we passed. "$720? Is that for real?"

The woman nodded. "That's actually one of the

least expensive pieces we have here. That one is Carmel Mission, and is 16" by 20". It's framed in a dark pewter molding and, personally, I think it's a steal."

"For $700, it had better be personally signed," Harry argued.

The attendant shook her head. "It isn't. But, we do have some which are. We do not have many left, I'm afraid, since Mr. Kinkade died in 2012."

"Oooo, look at this one, Zachary," Jillian exclaimed.

Turning, I saw my girlfriend staring at 24" by 36" print that had a very familiar landmark, namely, the covered walkway with 'Cannery Row' emblazoned across the front of it. It clearly depicted the local area, which explained why this particular shop had it for sale. Leaning close, I studied the illustration.

The vehicles in the illustration looked older, which, if I had to guess the year, would place it somewhere in the 1960s. It looked as though it had just rained, since I could see reflections of lights on the streets and the sidewalks. Then I read the display card that had been placed next to the painting and nodded. The picture, the artist explained, had been to commemorate Cannery Row's 50th Anniversary. Apparently, Mr. Kinkade had loved the feel of the area, with its coastal air, saturated with mists, and painted that into the picture.

"It's nice," I agreed.

"You haven't looked at the price yet," Jillian said, with a smile on her face.

"Why? Is it high?"

"That painting," the attendant hastily interrupted, "has been reprinted on premium canvas, hand-stretched across the wooden stretcher bars, and has been highlighted by a very skilled team of artisans. Do you see the 'PP' next to the title?"

I sighed when I heard Harry snicker.

"I do. What's it stand for?"

"Publisher Proof. Only a small number of prints are created with such detail."

"You're blocking the price," I said, as I looked at the female attendant. "Wow. Is it that bad?"

"I was just trying to explain why the price might be higher than you expect."

For the record, it was high, but surprisingly, it was lower than I had anticipated. I had thought the price would be in the neighborhood of at least ten grand. It was actually a shade below five. Grand, that is.

"Is this one signed?" I asked.

The attendant turned to the painting and pointed to the lower right corner.

"That's his signature, right there."

I squinted at the tiny, elegant script and, puzzled, looked up at the clerk.

"That's his signature? It looks like a stamp."

"That's because that is a stamp," the attendant clarified. She then tapped an area of the print about an inch or two north of the stamp. "His signature is here. He signed his name with a black pen. Does that help?"

I nodded. "I see it now. Thanks."

I glanced over at Jillian and saw her gazing admiringly at the print before moving off, heading deeper into the gallery. Once I was sure she was out of earshot, I moved closer to the attendant.

"I'll take it."

The attendant blinked her eyes a few times and stared at me.

"That," I said, pointing at the picture. "I said I'll take it. I mean, it is for sale, isn't it?"

Overhearing, Harry wandered closer. I noticed his presence and automatically handed him the leashes to the dogs.

"Well, yes, but ... wow. Okay, I don't think I've sold a print valued that high before."

I handed her a credit card and scribbled my home address on the back of one of Lentari Cellars' business cards.

"Please have it shipped here. It's a surprise for her. I don't want her knowing I've bought it, okay?"

The attendant took the card and turned it over. She read the name of my winery and her eyes lit up.

"Are you the owner of...?"

"Yes," I hastily interrupted, "and please keep your voice down. It's a surprise, remember?"

"Zachary?" Jillian called, from within the racks behind me, "you should see this one. Where are you?"

"I'll be right there," I called back, while looking at the attendant. Nodding, she hurriedly completed the transaction, swiped my card, and then printed out the receipt. I scribbled my name, took the receipt, and gave her my thanks.

"Where are you?" I called, as I moved deeper within the gallery.

"We're back here. There are some fantastic prints back here, and they're way more reasonable than the framed prints up front. Would you like to pick one out with me? If we buy two, then they'll throw in a free Thomas Kinkade blanket."

"Sure! I'm on my way."

"Dude, you already bought something," Harry whispered. "And, I can't believe you paid that much for a picture, man!"

"Quiet," I ordered. "Jillian loves art, and I, well, I love Jillian. I can afford it, so why not? What about Julie? Does she like art?"

Harry shook his head. "Nah. She never really got into this stuff, thank God."

"Oooo, look at this one!" I suddenly heard Julie exclaim. "It's gorgeous! We have a blank wall in our master bedroom that this would look fantastic on!"

Giving my friend a sly smile, and a nudge on his shoulder, we rounded the corner and rejoined the girls. Jillian was already halfway through one large bin full of plastic-encased prints. There were two other bins nearby. Smiling, I started flipping through prints as though I was looking through a box of vinyl records.

"I like this one," I said, as I pulled out a print.

There were small mountains covered by forests, a large, placid lake, and trees everywhere. I noticed that the trees were just starting to turn yellow, which meant the print depicted my favorite time of year: autumn.

"Coeur d'Alene," the attendant's voice said, from behind me. "That's one of my favorites, too. It's in northern Idaho. Have you ever been?"

The corners of my mouth turned upwards in a smile. "Once or twice. Jillian, what have you picked out?"

"Well, I'm trying to decide which one is my favorite between these two."

"Get them both," I suggested.

"Oh, I don't need to overindulge. Just one will do for me. I'll take this one."

I took the print Jillian pulled out and studied the scene. It was a picture-perfect setting, with a small stone cabin on the right, a smooth-as-glass river, and there was a canoe, pulled up onto the riverbank. A thin tendril of smoke could be seen, escaping the gray chimney. Directly in front of the small cabin was a fire pit, with a wooden bench nearby. Completing the image were several snow-capped mountains in the distance.

I nodded. "I like this one, too. Very nice."

"*Evening Majesty*," the attendant gushed. "That one is my absolute favorite. I have a signed print back home."

"You're lucky," Jillian told the woman, with a smile. "He's my favorite artist. I would have loved to own something from him that was signed."

Oh, you will, I thought, with a smile.

"Harry?" I prompted. "Do you need her help with your purchase?"

A blank look appeared on Harry's face.

"Huh?"

I gave him a hard look and shook my head. "Your purchase, amigo. Do you remember what we talked about out front?"

Harry suddenly nodded. "Oh, right. Yeah, man. I want to buy something, too."

Julie approached. "Oh? You do? Since when do you like art?"

"Uh, since ... well, you do, don't you? I wanna buy something for you. Which one would you like?"

The smile that appeared on Julie's face could have melted the coldest of hearts.

"Really? You want to buy me a print?"

Harry nodded. "You bet, Jules. Whichever one you want."

Jillian's eyebrows shot up. "Indeed?"

"That doesn't have a comma in the price tag," Harry quickly added.

With our purchases clutched tightly in our hands, we were just about to step outside the shop when someone's cell rang. In fact, I think it was mine. I passed the newly purchased prints to Jillian.

"Would you hold these for a second? I need to get my ... Sherlock? Watson? Hang on a sec, guys. I need to get my phone and can't do it if you're trying to pull me through the door. Hello?"

"Is this Mr. Zachary Anderson?"

"It is. Who is this?"

"Officer Marianne Adolphson. Do you remember me, Mr. Anderson?"

"Of course I do, Mary. We only met yesterday. And please, call me Zack. What's up?"

"We were wondering if you and your dogs would like to come down to the station and, er, help us out with something."

"Who is *we* and help you out with what, exactly?" I asked.

"The Monterey Police Department has invited you to come for a visit."

"No, they haven't," I chuckled. "They just want to meet Sherlock and Watson, don't they?"

I heard Mary laugh.

"Well, perhaps. As for your help, well, we were wondering if they could possibly lend their expertise on one of our cold cases."

"You do know that we're not going to be here that long, don't you?" I asked.

"I am aware. I made that point, and the captain doesn't think you'll be interested, but he does have an ace up his sleeve."

"And that would be...?"

"He wouldn't tell me. Will you come?"

"We'll be there within the hour."

* * *

Exactly 30 minutes later, the four of us ...oops. Did it again. The six of us were inside the Monterey Police Department headquarters, more specifically inside one of their conference rooms. All the cops were incredibly friendly and, much to my astonishment, not one of the cops gave us any flak for having solved so many police cases.

The captain, a stout gray-haired man about my age, was kind enough to show us around, and even filled us in on what had happened since yesterday. The woman we found hiding nearby, Sherry VanZanten, had been thoroughly questioned but then released, since as of right now, they were treating the death as an accident. They had notified Monterey Bay Aquarium and received a to-be-expected press release, lamenting the loss of their beloved aquarist and diver. When I asked about the second diver, the alleged diving buddy for the deceased, I was met with stony silence.

"There's still no word," Captain Owens admitted.

"What about the dive log, man?" Harry asked. "I thought I heard Mary say they were going to retrieve it from the aquarium?"

"We're due over there in less than an hour," Captain Owens confirmed. "We're meeting with the director of the aquarium, as well as the head of their PR department."

"What's this about asking for help on a cold case?" I wanted to know. "I have no problems helping you guys out. I mean, you've been nothing but nice to us the entire time we've been here. However, I have to point out the simple fact that we're heading home in a few days."

"If your dogs are as good as you say they are," the captain began, "then this should be a breeze."

"I never said anything of the sort," I protested.

Captain Owens waved a dismissive hand, "I know that. What I meant to say was, given all the rumors I've heard, your dogs should have plenty of time to recover it."

"Recover what?" I asked, a bit skeptically.

Captain Owens shrugged. "Some type of rare coin. It was Spanish, I think."

"From a treasure ship?" Harry eagerly asked.

"Off the California coast?" Captain Owens scoffed. "Unlikely. This belonged to a local collector. It was stolen almost a year ago and never turned up."

"I hate to say it," I slowly began, "but that thing is probably long gone by now. The thief probably sold it on eBay."

"It's possible," Captain Owens admitted. "However, the owner is a Council member, and never fails to ask me how his case is going whenever he sees me. And, it pains me to admit that I see that smug bastard more often than I'd like."

"What makes you think I can find this missing coin?" I stammered.

"I don't. I think your dogs might have a fighting chance, though."

"Fine. What makes you think Sherlock and Watson can find this coin?"

"If the coin is still in Monterey, then I'll bet your dogs can find it. Let's face it, they found that Egyptian necklace, didn't they?"

"The time involved was much less than it is here," Jillian clarified. "The pendant was stolen and recovered in less than a week. You're telling us that this coin was stolen almost a year ago?"

"All I'm asking is you try," Captain Owens explained. "All right, look. If you decide to try, and end up actually finding this coin, then the MPD will personally pick up the tab for your hotel stay."

I was silent as I considered. Mistaking my silence as negative, the captain continued.

"For all of you."

I heard a grunt of surprise from Harry.

"Dude, that's over seven hundred bucks! Apiece! Come on, man. You've got to let 'em try. What do you say, Zack?"

Seven hundred bucks, while significant, wasn't going to break me, and I was tempted to just turn down the captain, regardless of how eager Harry had become. However, one look at Jillian had me reconsidering. My girlfriend had squatted next to the dogs so that she could drape an arm around each of them.

"You two are the cutest, smartest dogs in the

whole world, aren't you?"

Both corgis panted happily.

"I'll bet you could find that coin, couldn't you?"

Sherlock licked Jillian's hand, as if to say, 'Challenge accepted.' For whatever reason, it would seem Jillian wanted to look for this coin. I glanced over at Harry and Julie, who were talking animatedly between themselves. And, for once they weren't arguing, but talking excitedly. That could only be a good thing. Who was I to muck up everyone's fun?

"Okay, we'll do it. But, no guarantees."

Captain Owens nodded appreciatively. He handed me a slip of paper.

"This is his name and address. He's expecting you."

"How did you even know we'd agree to do this?"

"I didn't," Captain Owens admitted. "Up until five minutes ago, I thought I was going to have to call Chet back up and tell him it wasn't going to happen. However, I have faith in your dogs. Good luck, Mr. Anderson."

Fifteen minutes later, we were all piled in a ridesharing van, headed for the home of this Monterey coin collector. Yes, I could have pulled Jillian's SUV out of valet parking at our hotel, but this seemed easier. I looked over at my girlfriend and grinned.

"Bet you didn't think we'd be doing this when

you suggested we go on a road trip vacation last week, did you?"

"Not at all," Jillian admitted. "That's what makes it so fun!"

"You're really enjoying this, aren't you?" I asked, amazed.

"Of course. I've always loved visiting Monterey. In fact, after listening to you and Harry talk about diving, I think I want to take it up."

"Take what up? Scuba diving? Are you sure?"

"It sounds like so much fun. There are tons of places to dive off the Oregon coast. Besides, I'd love to be your diving partner."

"Umm, about that," I began.

"What is it?" Jillian asked. "Are you still able to dive?"

"It's not that," I said, shaking my head. "It's ... well, I haven't dived for so long that I would need to take a refresher course."

Jillian took my hands in hers and squeezed them.

"That's perfect, Zachary! We can learn it together!"

"We're in!" Julie enthusiastically added. "That does sound like a lot of fun. We'll join you, won't we, dear?"

I looked over at Harry and saw a concerned look on his face.

"What's the matter?" I asked. "You haven't dived in a while, either? No problem. We can all take the class together."

"You're forgetting what we have to do before the class would start," Harry grumped. "Provided they still do the swimming test."

"Hey, I'm the one who had a difficult time treading water," I reminded my friend. I looked at Jillian and gave her a sheepish grin. "I sink like a rock when I'm in a pool."

"Don't you want to get your certification again?" Julie asked, as she looked at her husband. "Don't you think it'd be fun?"

"Not for me," Harry sulked.

"And why not?" I asked.

"Wetsuits, bro. We'd have to wear wetsuits."

"Yeah, we would," I agreed. "I've felt how cold the water can be. There's no way I'm getting in it without a wetsuit."

"Dude, I won't fit in a wetsuit."

"Is that what you're worried about?" I asked. "You want to lose some weight, is that it?"

"I'm out of shape, man. It wouldn't be any fun for me."

I watched Julie's face fall. Jillian squeezed my hand and looked imploringly into my eyes, begging me to do something. Swallowing my pride, I cleared my throat and waited for Harry to look at me.

"Okay, here's what we do. Next spring, when it starts getting nice out, we're all getting certified."

"But I told you ..." Harry protested.

"Let me finish," I interrupted. "In the meantime, I suggest you and I get into shape. There's a perfectly acceptable gym in town. I say we both join."

"But, you don't need to work out," Harry insisted. "You're not the one with a gut the size of mine."

"That's because I don't drink as much as you," I reminded my friend. "Besides, it could never hurt to tone up. If you're serious about wanting to dive with us, then tell me now. I'll be your workout partner. We're both going to want to look good in wetsuits, so ... Jillian? Are you okay?"

"I hadn't thought about the wetsuits," Jillian admitted.

"Neither had I," Julie echoed.

"Are you changing your mind?" I asked.

Jillian shook her head. "Heavens no. Michael never liked the water, so we didn't take too many trips here as a couple. Perhaps that's why I'm looking forward to this as much as I am. Those wetsuits, are they as revealing as I think they are?"

Both Harry and I nodded.

"They're skin tight and magnify every flaw that you have," I gravely told her. "Trust me, they look much better on women than they do on men."

"Well, then I'll join the gym with you," Jillian decided.

"We both will," Julie added.

I looked over at Harry.

"There. We're all going. That should make you feel better, right?"

"It does, thanks. I'm sorry, bro. I shouldn't be laying all this on you. You guys don't have to join the gym just because I'm a pudgy dude."

"No worries, Harry," I assured my friend. "No worries."

Ten minutes later, we were standing in front of the coin collector's home. The house this guy owned was nothing short of a mansion. Here was a guy, I decided, that had a few bucks to rub together. Granted, both Jillian and I were doing quite well, and I'm almost certain my girlfriend's checkbook would make even this guy's pale in comparison, but did she live as lavishly as this? I mean, there's a Ferrari parked in the drive, for Pete's sake. In fact, it looked just like the one Tom Selleck drove while he played the part of Magnum, P.I.

"Nice wheels," Harry observed.

"Too pretentious for me," Jillian softly told me.

"I don't think I'd fit," I decided, eliciting a giggle from the girls.

"Think all you want, man," Harry said. "I know I wouldn't fit. That's it. I accept. I'll go to the gym with you guys."

"It also means cutting out a lot of the food you like to munch on," Julie sternly warned him. "Chips, cookies, and all those little fun-sized candy bars at the clinic will have to go."

"Or exercise a little more self-control and don't touch 'em," I added, with a grin.

"You're enjoying this," Harry accused.

"Julie hasn't even hit the beverage side of the equation yet," I pointed out.

Julie snapped her fingers. "That's right! No more beer for you, Harrison."

"You shut your filthy little mouth!" Harry snapped.

The three of us fell silent. Was he serious? Then I caught sight of Harry's face. He was grinning and only had eyes for Julie. His wife grunted once, shook her head, and then slugged him on the arm. Hard.

"Doofus. This will be good for both of us."

"I'm not sure how the kids will take to the new diet," Harry said, adopting a serious tone.

"You leave the kids out of this," Julie told Harry. "They're kids. Let them be kids."

"What a load of crap," Harry remarked. "Hardy is in high school now, and Drew is, what? Almost eight? Yeah, okay. That's a little young. Just Hardy, then."

"No," Julie contradicted. "Leave them out of it. We'll do this ourselves. Nice, healthy meals with plenty of fruits and vegetables."

Harry groaned and shoved his hands into his pockets. At that time, the front door opened and an older man, tall and lean, walked up to us. His skin was darkened by the sun, which suggested he spent an inordinate amount of time outdoors. When he shook hands, I could feel how heavily calloused it was. Whatever this guy did to make his money, it had to have been something that kept him outside and working with his hands.

"Chet Mayberry. I'm pleased to meet you all. And would these two be the famous Sherlock and Watson I've heard so much about?"

"They are," I confirmed. "Sherlock has some black on him, while Watson is red and white."

Chet nodded. "Got it. Well, you've all come this far. Come in! Come in! We'll get you out of the hot sun and I can tell you all about my collection."

"You have a lovely home," Jillian said, as we all stepped inside the mansion. "I love your foyer. It's very impressive."

Jillian was definitely right. The foyer had a white marble floor, with several black marble pedestals in various places, and on those pedestals were white statues. I could only imagine that they were made of marble, too. This guy clearly liked his marble.

Twin staircases, spiraling up to the second floor, were on either side of the foyer. Glancing up, I could see that the staircases kept going up, connecting to what looked like a third landing, and possibly a fourth, although I couldn't quite tell at this angle.

"This is very nice," Harry commented, as we all followed Chet inside the house. "Love the wheels out front, man. Makes me think Magnum is in here somewhere."

Chet grinned. "It's funny you should say that. That particular car was one of the cars actually driven by Tom Selleck while he was filming in Hawaii. It's a 1984 Ferrari 308 GTS, and it has less than 40,000 miles on it. I love it."

I looked at Chet and cleared my throat.

"If you don't mind me asking," I hesitantly began, "but how do you fit in that thing? You look as though you're as tall as me. I know I have a few pounds on you..."

"...a few?" Harry snorted.

"Do you really want to go there?" Julie whispered back, annoyed.

Harry promptly fell silent.

"...but I think there's no way I'd fit in it."

"Probably not," Chet admitted. "As for me, well, it's uncomfortable to drive. Not much leg room, I'm sorry to say."

"Yet Tom Selleck drove it," I insisted. "I always wanted to know how he did that."

"They had to modify the Ferraris he drove," Chet explained. "They removed padding, so the seats were lower, and speaking of the seats, they were bolted in place as far back as possible, to give him more leg room. Even so, if you ever go back to watch the series, you'll see that he rarely drove with the top up."

"You learn something new each day," I admitted, as I grinned at our new friend.

I was really starting to like this Chet person. He was really easy-going, easy to talk to, and he had a car from Magnum, P.I.! I wonder if I could canoodle a test drive out of him. I'd have to inquire later. For the time being, we were here to talk about a missing coin.

Right on cue, we entered a room the size of my living room. Glass display cases were everywhere, including along every inch of available wall space. There were even several cases set back-to-back down the length of the room, allowing even more of Chet's personal collection of coins to be displayed.

"Welcome to my coin room. Please, feel free to look around."

Whistling appreciatively, I took Jillian's hand and slowly walked along the row of cases on my right. Chet appeared next to me and began spewing facts about each of the coins.

"That one is a 1922 St. Gauden Gold Double Eagle. It's been graded MS64."

"Worth a lot?" I guessed.

Chet shrugged. "Maybe $1,800. Oh, do you see this one here? Have you ever seen what an authentic Spanish doubloon looks like?"

The four of us crowded around the display. Sherlock and Watson, content to be near us, settled to the ground to wait. Chet produced a set of keys, tapped in a code on a keypad on the side of the case, and unlocked the cabinet. He reached in to retrieve the gold coin.

"Umm, shouldn't you be wearing a glove?" I hesitantly asked.

"Protective case," Chet answered, as he handed the coin to me. "This is a 1792 Madrid 1 Escudo

Charles IV doubloon."

"Sweet," Harry said, as I handed him the coin. "How much is it worth?"

"That one? Oh, about $400."

"That it?" Harry asked, as he frowned. "I would've thought it'd be more, man."

"You can't place value on a coin just by its appearance," Chet informed us. He placed the coin back in the cabinet and relocked it. He guided us to a case on the opposite wall and tapped the glass directly over an empty spot on one of the shelves. "This is what you people are here for. I'm really hoping you might be able to retrieve my missing Reales for me."

"You're missing what?" I asked, confused. "What is a ray-all?"

"It's Spanish," Chet explained. "This one was a 1721 Spanish Silver 2 Reales coin. It was in fantastic condition. All the little intricate details I love about old colonial coins were still there. Truth be told, it was one of the first coins I ever found."

"And you found all of these?" Julie exclaimed. She nodded. "Okay, now I'm impressed."

Chet laughed. "No, I only found perhaps a fifth of them. The rest I bought off of other collectors, or at auctions, and so on."

"How much is this really worth?" I asked. "Is it the most valuable coin in your collection?"

"Psssht," Chet snorted. "Not even close. This one was probably worth about $400."

"That's it?" I demanded. "An authentic 18th

century coin is only worth $400? Wow. I spend more than that on her champagne."

Jillian shrugged. "True story, I'm afraid. What can I say? I like my Crystal Rose."

As I mentioned, Crystal Rose was a very expensive champagne that just so happened to be Jillian's favorite. Yes, it retails for $400, but once you add in the sales tax, well, it pushes the final bill to around $440. But, does that stop me? No. It's Jillian's favorite, so I have a bottle or two stashed back in the winery for those special occasions. I also have one being delivered here, but I'll go more into that later.

"I don't get it," Harry complained. "Why would someone steal this one coin and leave all the others behind?"

"Maybe he didn't have the others when this one was stolen?" I suggested. "Which brings me to my next question. How long ago did this happen?"

"The theft? Oh, gosh, this was nearly ... eight months ago."

"Eight months ago?" I repeated, shaking my head. "The MPD made it sound like this happened years ago."

"They would," Chet laughed. "Look, this is Monterey. Nothing much happens here. For the locals, eight months is a long time. I'm honestly surprised they brought you people all the way down here. They must be getting desperate."

"I think you misunderstand," Jillian said. "We weren't brought specifically down from Oregon.

We're on vacation. The police just so happen to be fans of the dogs, and know how skilled they are in solving cases."

"Ah, and they want to see if the famous Sherlock and Watson can find my coin, is that it?"

Jillian nodded. "Exactly. However, as Zachary stated earlier, we're not in town for that long, so I don't know what we'd be able to do that the local police haven't done already."

Chet shrugged. "Hey, if you get lucky, fantastic. That particular coin holds sentimental value to me, so I'd love to get it back. However, if you can't, well, c'est la vie, I suppose. I'll just have to make do without it."

Jillian cleared her throat. "Could you tell us which display held your coin? Do you have any ideas who might have taken it?"

Chet nodded, and turned to point at the display farthest from the door. "Of course. That one there. Let me show you."

We all followed the friendly collector over to a large glass display case, which was currently holding a wide variety of coins.

"Do you see the lower left corner and the empty holder? I had that coin displayed there for several years."

"How many people do you bring in here?" I asked.

Chet shrugged. "Oh, gosh, that's a hard question to answer. Hundreds. On more than one occasion, I have let local school groups in here, I've hosted tours, and entertained other collectors on more than one occasion."

"Do you have any suspicions?" Jillian asked.

Chet shook his head. "No, I'm sorry to say. It could have been stolen by any number of people."

I felt a tug on Sherlock's leash. Looking down, I saw that both dogs were looking back, at the door. Clearly, both corgis wanted to leave. Did they already have an idea where to go? I nudged Jillian and looked down at the dogs. She gave me an affirmative nod.

"I have one final question before we go," I said, as I felt the dogs tug on the leash a second time. "You said this coin is nowhere close to your most valuable, right?"

Chet nodded. "That's right. Why? Do you want to know which is the most valuable? I can show you, if you'd like."

I pulled the dogs to a stop and eagerly nodded. "I would, yeah. Thanks. Sherlock? Watson? Come on, you two. We're almost done here, then you can see if you can work some of your magic, okay?"

Sherlock snorted and turned to follow Chet back into the coin room. Our host walked directly to the row of cases in the middle of the room and stopped at the center. He tapped the glass and gazed lovingly at the sole occupant of the case. To me, it looked like a golden silver dollar. I also noticed that the glass in this case differed from the others. A closer inspection revealed it to be at least an inch thick.

"Don't get too close," Chet warned. "This baby has some heavy-duty, anti-theft precautions in place."

"What's in there?" Julie asked.

"What you're looking at," Chet explained, "is a 1715 Royal, made for the king at the time, Phillip V. A handful were made, and only a few have ever been found. Think of it as the Holy Grail of numismatology. This, my friends, is the Tricentennial Royal."

"And, uh, how much is it worth?" Harry hesitantly asked.

"Well, I ended up paying nearly $300,000 for it a few years ago, and I think I got a bargain. It's worth at least double that now."

I held my hands up in a time-out gesture.

"Wait just a minute. You're telling me that someone passed up a coin worth over half a million dollars to steal one that was less than a thousand?"

Chet shrugged. "I can't explain it, either."

"Something doesn't add up," I said, as I turned to Jillian. My girlfriend was nodding, too. "Chet, it's been a pleasure. If we find your coin, then we'll let you know, okay?"

"I couldn't ask for anything else," the coin collector said, grinning.

He shook each of our hands as we headed outside. The four of us were silent, each lost to our own thoughts, while we waited for the rideshare Jillian ordered to arrive. Why in the world would a thief willingly pass up a coin worth many thousands more than the one they ended up stealing? What was so important about that coin?

And why, all of a sudden, were the dogs restless? Could it be that the corgis were anxious to begin their search? Thinking of the money I'd save if the dogs located Chet's missing coin, I grinned. That would be more than enough to buy another few bottles of Jillian's pricey bubbly.

FOUR

Later that afternoon, we were back at the waterfront. Once again, I was holding the towels, since this time, we were encouraging the dogs to go into the water. Both of them were still restless, and I was hoping some good, old-fashioned exercise would take some of the edge off. For all you corgi owners out there, you'll back me up. If your dog, who is already highly active to begin with, exhibits signs that they could possibly wear a path in the linoleum, then it's time to get them outside to burn off some of that energy.

So far, it seemed to be working. Just as soon as we made it back to the hotel, I changed into swimming trunks and a tank top (I had no intentions of going into the water, but to be safe, in case one of the dogs needed help, I was going to be prepared). We checked in on Harry and Julie, but saw a Do Not Disturb sign on their door, so we left them alone. With leashes in hand, we headed back to the beach, and thankfully, this was where the dogs seemed to be wanting to go. Walking along the waterfront once more, while watching the dogs' antics, I decided to multitask and again, found myself staring at the ground, looking for bits of glass. Finding a few that fit the parameters Jillian had previously laid out, I gathered them up.

"Do you need any more green pieces?" I asked, as I studied a quarter-sized, slightly curved piece of dark green glass I had found.

Jillian studied the piece and eventually nodded. "I have a few others already, but let's keep this one, just in case. I like the shape of it."

I pulled out the resealable sandwich bag I had in my pocket and dropped in the piece. That's when I heard a splash. Turning, I saw Sherlock swimming steadily away from shore.

"What do you think you're doing? Get back here, you goofball!"

I heard Sherlock snort, then turn around so that he was looking at me. Bear in mind, he was about twenty feet away from shore, just lazily floating on the water. Somehow, that little booger knew I couldn't float on the water like he could, and he was taunting me with it.

"Don't aggravate the person who feeds you, pal," I warned the feisty corgi. "You'd better not make me get wet."

Sherlock snorted again and then easily swam back to shore.

"What's with you, pal? Why would you ... ack! *Pbttth!* Don't shake yourself off next to me! Why you little snot. That's it. You're asking for it."

Now, I should point out that, for all intents and

purposes, I was acting as if I was mad. I wasn't. Sherlock and I played like this all the time back home. This was me, signaling to him, that I intended to chase his furry butt. Sherlock, for his part, immediately crouched low and wiggled his stub of a tail. He yipped a challenge, as if to say, Come and get me, lardball.

I tossed the towels over at Jillian, who was giggling uncontrollably as she wrestled with her purse to find her phone. Knowing her, she's gonna record this and share it with others at the most inopportune time in the future. Whatever. I really didn't care.

I took off after Sherlock, who yipped once, turned tail, and bolted in the opposite direction. Watson, not wanting to be left out, suddenly raced by me, on a direct line which would have her intercept her packmate well before I could get there. Together, the two corgis then turned right, raced toward me, as though they were playing chicken, and then turned away again at the last possible moment.

Those little pups were still taunting me! They knew I'd never be able to catch them. Oh, yeah? Two can play this game.

I immediately turned in the other direction and sprinted away. I then heard twin barks of annoyance and, suddenly, two sleek forms zipped by me. Realizing I was now chasing the dogs again, I reversed course one more time and took off, back the way we had just come.

Sherlock barked again. This time, I could hear the exasperated tones in his bark. What happened next, I'm sorry to say, would make me the featured video of the day on YouTube. Sherlock came racing up behind me and nudged my left heel with his snout. It was just enough to push my left foot into the path of my right, and down I went. Hard. And, since I had been running, my mouth was wide open.

Thankfully, there was sand everywhere, and I was spared any physical injury. It didn't help my ego, though, as I rolled to my knees and spat out a mouthful of sand. Ever have sand in your mouth? How about an entire mouthful?

I glared at Sherlock, who was sitting next to me with an amused expression on his face. Watson, for her part, had cuddled up next to me, as though she thought I had been hurt. And that's when I saw her. Jillian, my wonderful girlfriend, had her phone out and was recording. Plus, she was laughing so hard she had tears running down her face.

"Thaks a lop," I told her, as I tried valiantly to get every grain of sand out of my mouth. "*Blech*. Did you record all that?"

Jillian passed me her water bottle and nodded her tear-streaked face.

With my mouth properly rinsed, I turned back to the dogs, but noticed they were no longer there. Judging by the tracks in the sand, they had wandered around a group of large rocks and were, presumably, back at the water's edge. Curious as to what they were doing, I made it four steps when I heard the chirps and coos. It was the otters. Apparently, the corgis were otter-watching again. They were standing, motionless, at the extreme edge of the shore and were staring out at the open ocean.

"I think our otter friends are back," I said, as I took Jillian's hand. "Come on, I want to chaperone them. I don't want them enticing Sherlock to come into the water to play with them."

I heard the splash and cursed mightily. Jillian and I hurried to the water's edge and skidded to a stop. I had just started to pull my tank top up when Jillian laid a hand on mine to stop me.

"Look, Zachary. You were right. They're playing!"

Sherlock was swimming steadily in circles as the otters danced through the water. Furry heads would pop up less than a foot from Sherlock's head, we would hear a soft chirp, and by the time Sherlock looked in that direction, the otter would already be gone.

Relaxing somewhat, I took Jillian's hand and, together, we made for the closest rock that was suitable for sitting. After a few moments, I wrapped my arm around her waist. Jillian snuggled closer as we watched the antics in the water.

"I like it here," I said, in a soft tone. "And I have to tell you, I'm really looking forward to getting my scuba certification again."

"I'm glad, Zachary. I think we'll have a lot of fun together."

I thought about the bottle of Crystal Rose that was due to arrive in two days at the hotel and shook my head. I never thought I'd be this content again. Or this happy. You know what they say about lightning, right? That it never strikes the same place twice? I used to think that about love as well. I never would have imagined I could feel this way again. Just to think, as little as two years ago, I was pining away, in Phoenix, alone and miserable. And now? I'm with a beautiful woman. I own a winery that my late wife, Samantha, would be proud of, and have two corgis who adore me.

I thought back to the sand in my mouth and grunted. Well, at least one does. Watson, sensing my thoughts, nuzzled up against my leg and looked up at me.

"I'm just teasing. I know you both love me." I looked over at Jillian and saw that she was studying the bay. I gave her shoulder a friendly squeeze. When she looked over at me, I smiled. "Penny for your thoughts."

"I was just thinking about my parents."

"Oh? What about them? They should be back home by now, shouldn't they?"

Jillian nodded. "They are. I texted them earlier to see when they'd arrive, and they informed me that they cut their last stop out of the trip and had already arrived home."

"Oh? Why's that?"

"I think it's because they've been gone for over two years now. Seriously, would you want to live in an RV for that long?"

"I would, as long as you were there with me," I automatically answered.

Jillian gave me a kiss on the cheek and laid her head on my shoulder.

"Good answer, Zachary. Good answer."

I heard a whine and, looking down, I saw that Watson was still staring at me.

"Fine. That goes for you two as well. Wow. Two years, huh? That's a long time."

"They did travel all across North America," Jillian pointed out. "And even up into Canada."

"They must truly love to travel."

"My mother does," Jillian corrected.

"And your father?" I prompted. "He doesn't?"

"Not so much."

"What does your father like to do?"

"To see my mother happy," Jillian said, with a giggle.

"Did they manage to hit every state like they said they wanted?" I asked.

"All but Hawaii, obviously. And, they even visited all ten provinces in Canada."

"Wow. So, that means they went to Alaska, too?"

Jillian nodded. "Yes. They liked it so well that they stayed for a full month in Anchorage."

"I liked Anchorage," I said, thinking back to my trip up north. "Beautiful city. Rugged scenery. Loved the mountains you could see south of the city. You're going to love it."

"I can't wait for our cruise!" Jillian exclaimed. "Just think, we'll be there next summer, in June! A cruise up the Inside Passage. It'll be ..."

"... romantic?" I finished for her, after she trailed off.

"Well, yes, but that wasn't what I was going to say. I was thinking, it'll be breathtaking."

"Due to the temperatures," I guessed. "I wonder how cold it'll be?"

"I was referring to the raw beauty," Jillian corrected. "Alaska is the biggest state in the country, and yet has one of the lowest populations. I can't wait to see it!"

"I'm looking forward to it," I assured her.

The ring of my cell phone shattered the tranquility of the moment. Sighing, I pulled out my phone and looked at the display. While not recognizing the number, I did recognize the area code. Someone from Monterey was calling me.

"Hello?"

"Is this Zachary Anderson?"

"It is. Who's this?"

"Officer Marianne Adolphson."

"Hello, Mary. How's it going? What can I do for you?"

"I thought you'd like to know ... we received an official response from the aquarium."

"About that guy's death? How'd that go?"

"They expressed remorse, obviously, but something about their attitude is ... I don't know."

I couldn't help it. "Fishy?" I guessed.

"Yes, that's it," Mary laughed. "Listen, I was about ready to head over there to talk to the director. He's expecting me in about thirty minutes. Being an official police consultant for Pomme Valley, and since you're the one who discovered the body, I have permission to invite you along, if you'd like."

"Just a moment. Let me ask Jillian."

"Of course."

I muted the call and turned to Jillian.

"It's Mary, from the police. She's inviting us to accompany her to talk to the guys at the aquarium. Do you want to go?"

Jillian nodded. "Sure. But, I think you're forgetting something."

"What's that?"

Jillian looked over at Sherlock, who was still swimming in the water, cavorting with the playful otters. She then looked down at Watson and scratched behind her ears.

"We can't leave the dogs here."

"We can take them with us," I argued.

Jillian shook her head. "Not into an aquarium, we can't. There's no way they'd allow pets in there."

"Hey, bro," a familiar voice suddenly said. "There you are. We've been looking for you."

Harry and Julie appeared, looking somewhat disheveled, if you ask me. I gave my friend a sly grin. Julie noticed the look Harry and I gave each other and blushed.

"Perfect timing, pal," I said, as Jillian and I rose to our feet. "I need you to dog sit for us."

Harry nodded. "Sure. Where're you headed? Did the dogs find a lead in the cold coin case?"

"Cold coin case," I scoffed, chuckling. "No. That's fairly low on the totem pole. If Sherlock happens to find the coin, great. However, right now, we're headed to the aquarium. The police invited us to talk with the aquarium bigwigs about the death of their star diver."

"We'd love to take care of your dogs for you," Julie told us. She looked left, then right. "Umm, I see Watson. Where's Sherlock?"

I tossed the towels to Harry and pointed at the water. "Sherlock is over there, swimming with some otters. You'll need to thoroughly dry him off when he comes out. Thanks, pal!"

"What?" Harry sputtered, as he stared at the towels. "I don't wanna ... you owe me!"

Thirty minutes later, Jillian and I were strolling through the front entrance of the world-famous Monterey Bay Aquarium. This facility opened in 1984 and has won numerous awards for their exhibition of wildlife, their conservation efforts, and their educational programs. The non-profit facility draws around two million visitors a year and has to be the most visited aquarium in the country.

"I've always loved coming here," Jillian told me, as we took a seat just inside the front entrance, at the Membership and Tours section.

"I can see why. I really like the layout. I mean, look at that over there. The sign says, Kelp Forest. I've seen kelp before, but good grief, I didn't know it grew that tall."

"It says it can get up to 28 feet tall," Jillian said.

"Where's it say that?" I wanted to know.

Jillian pointed at the large tank, visible through the open doorway.

"Right there, next to the Kelp Forest sign."

"I need to have my eyes checked," I grumbled. "I see the sign you're talking about, but don't have a chance of reading that from this distance."

Five minutes later, Officer Adolphson appeared, in full uniform. She spotted us sitting on one of the benches and strolled over.

"Mr. Anderson, Ms. Cooper, thank you for joining me."

"Is Officer Lewis not joining us today?" Jillian asked, as she looked behind Mary to see if she could spot any other police officers.

"Nope, it's just me today. Had I been making an arrest, or executing a warrant, then I'd have backup. As it is, a simple meeting doesn't necessitate any additional manpower."

"Yet, you called us," I reminded her.

Mary shrugged. "It was the captain's idea. Personally, I think he didn't want me to go alone."

"That's nice," Jillian decided. "Or condescending, I haven't decided which yet."

"That makes two of us," Mary agreed, sounding a little cross. "Anyway, are we ready to go in? I see two staff members headed our way."

We rose to our feet just as two people--an older man wearing a blue polo shirt emblazoned with the aquarium's logo on the upper left breast pocket and khaki pants, and a woman--approached. He looked to be slightly older than I was and had black hair with just a few touches of gray. The woman accompanying him was in her late twenties, had short, curly brown hair, and wore a similar outfit, only her shirt was green. As I had noticed with our coin-collecting friend, Chet, both staff members sported dark tans, as though they spent a great deal of time outdoors.

"Jonathan Hawk," the man said, by way of introducing himself. "I'm director of the aquarium. This is Heather Rasmussen. She's head of Human Resources. Thank you for meeting with us."

"On behalf of the Monterey Police Department, thank you for having us," Mary formally responded. "I'm Officer Marianne Adolphson. This is Zack Anderson and Jillian Cooper. Both are from Pomme Valley, Oregon. Zack is a police consultant, and just so happened to be the person who spotted the body in the water."

The director held out an arm, indicating we should head farther into the aquarium.

"Please, let's talk somewhere a little more private, shall we?"

"You're from Pomme Valley?" Heather asked, as we headed past the Mission to the Deep sign and then past the Kelp Forest exhibit. "I've been up there a few times. They've got some great wine up there."

"They do, indeed," Jillian agreed. "If you don't mind me asking, which one is your favorite?"

"Oh, gosh. There are so many. I think I'd have to say that Syrah is my favorite."

"Do you have a favorite winery?" Jillian pressed.

Heather nodded. "I do. It's a different sounding name, so I'm not sure if I'm remembering it correctly. There's something about cellars in the title."

At this, I stopped and turned to look at their head of HR.

"Cellars? As in, Lentari Cellars?"

Heather snapped her fingers. "That's it. You've heard of it?"

I nodded. "You could say that. I own it."

Our group came to a sudden stop. The director turned to me, with skepticism written all over his face, and placed a hand on my shoulder.

"You're telling me you're the owner of the finest wine I've ever tasted outside of Italy?"

"I'll pass that on to Caden, my winemaster," I promised, as I gave Mr. Hawk a grin. "The only thing I'm responsible for is writing the checks."

"You ought to know, we serve your wine in our restaurant, Mr. Anderson."

"I had no idea," I confessed. "And please, call me Zack."

"Well, Zack, I may need to talk to you once this unfortunate business is all over. We're thinking about opening another restaurant at our facility, and naturally, we'd like to feature your wine. Perhaps some type of trade could be arranged?"

I nodded. "I'm sure we can work something out, Mr. Hawk."

"If I have to call you Zack, then you can call me Jon."

"Got it." I nodded. "Will do, Jon."

The five of us headed through a large set of glass doors, emerging outside. Jon steered us toward what was labeled as a Wildlife Viewing Station and brought us to a stop. We were now facing west, overlooking the mighty Pacific Ocean. Down below us, to our left, was what the staff called their Great Tide Pool. As I stood there, staring down at the thousands and thousands of gallons of water, I got a strange sense of recognition.

"What's the matter?" Jillian suddenly asked. "You're frowning."

"I've seen this before," I told my girlfriend. I swept my arm across the pool and shook my head. "I just don't know how or where."

"At the movies," Jon said, grinning.

I turned to the director. "Hmm? What was that?"

"The Great Tide Pool. It's been featured in films, but most notably, this was the home of George and Gracie, two humpback whales..."

"...from Star Trek IV," I finished. "Thanks, pal.

That would have driven me nuts. Wow. It was really filmed here?"

"The whales weren't real, of course," Jon said.

"It was just some Hollywood magic," Heather added.

Mary cleared her throat. She was holding a small notebook in one hand and a pen in the other.

"Could I ask you some questions about Mr. Jack Carlton now?"

Jon nodded. "Of course. As our press release stated, we at MBA are incredibly saddened by this loss. Jack Carlton was a truly gifted scuba diver, aquarist, and conservationist, and will be missed by all."

Now, I may not have a photographic memory, but that certainly sounded like it was, word-for-word, identical to what was on the aforementioned press release. I glanced over at Heather, and saw what I thought to be a look of regret pass over her features. I squeezed Jillian's hand, and when she was looking at me, nodded in Heather's direction.

"Is it true that Mr. Carlton only worked here part-time?" Mary continued.

Jon nodded. "That's correct. He divided his time between us, the east coast, New Zealand, and London."

"Was he associated with any institutions in New Zealand or England?"

Jon shrugged, and looked expectantly at Heather.

"No, he wasn't," Heather answered.

"Then why did he spend so much time there?" I asked.

"That's where he was paid to go," Heather said, shrugging.

"Paid by whom?" Mary wanted to know.

"National Geographic. He was one of their top divers. They sent him all around the globe. From what Jack told us, they usually sent him to either Wellington or London."

"Do you know where he was sent last?" Mary asked, scribbling furiously.

Heather looked at Jon. "Wasn't it somewhere in South America? Venezuela, I think."

"I don't know," Jon admitted. "If you check his dive log, I'm sure it'd tell you where he dove last."

"I'm glad you brought that up," Mary said, as she finished writing notes. She looked up at the director. "We're going to need to see his dive log. We need to know where he was diving, and most importantly, who he was diving with."

"Logs," Heather corrected. "He has at least five thick diving logs. That's how much Jack loved the water."

"How well did you know him?" Mary asked. "You keep referring to him as Jack and not Mr. Carlton."

Heather blushed. "Oh, umm, not that well, really. I mean ..."

The head of HR trailed off as she noticed the disapproving frown on Jon's face.

"Did the two of you have something going on?" Jon coolly asked, using a neutral tone of voice.

I blinked with surprise. The director's question, while not accusatory nor derogatory, seemingly dropped the ambient temperature in the area by at least thirty degrees. I'm surprised my breath didn't come out in visible puffs of air.

"That was a long time ago," Heather reluctantly admitted. "I've moved on."

"Why didn't I know anything about this?" Jon demanded.

"Because it would have been frowned upon," Heather said, with a sigh.

"Damn right," Jon snapped. He suddenly remembered he wasn't alone and looked over at the three of us and let out a sheepish grin. "I apologize. You shouldn't have had to witness that. As I was saying, if you want to know where *Mr. Carlton* dove," Jon continued, throwing the tiniest bit of emphasis on the proper way to refer to the deceased, "then you'll have to get your hands on those log books."

"Where are they now?" Mary asked.

"They should be in his office," Jon stated. He pointed back the way they had come. "It's this way. I'll take you to them."

"We appreciate your cooperation," Mary was saying. "While we're headed toward the deceased's office, let me ask you a question."

"Go ahead," Jon said, as he held open the glass door and waited for the four of us to reenter the building.

"Volunteers. How many volunteers does the aquarium actually have?"

Jon looked back at Heather. "Ms. Rasmussen, would you care to field this one?"

"Of course," Heather quickly said. "At any time, the aquarium has nearly a thousand volunteers."

I whistled with amazement. "Wow! Really? That's incredible."

"Each of our aquarists usually has one or two dedicated volunteers," Heather continued, "who would help that staff member maintain their exhibits."

Jillian suddenly nodded. "Let me venture a guess. Mr. Carlton had more, didn't he?"

"He had a very dedicated five or six," Heather confirmed. "In addition, he was the only aquarist on staff who had a waiting list of people wanting to volunteer for him."

"And why's that?" I wanted to know. "Was this guy that popular? Seriously, all I can think about now is that Dos Equis commercial. You know, it's the series of commercials which featured The Most Popular Man in the World?"

Heather smiled briefly. "I know the ones you mean. However, it isn't true, since ... well, let me rephrase. Depending on how you look at it, it could be. Jack, er, Mr. Carlton, was known for making trips all over the world."

"You guys mentioned that," I recalled.

"His work has been featured in magazines and

he has had a hand in filming numerous specials."

My eyebrows shot up. "Really? That's impressive."

Heather nodded. "If you wanted to get your toe in the door of an animal husbandry career, then having Jack Carlton on your side would be the ultimate reference."

I grunted. "If that isn't a reason to volunteer for someone, then I don't know what is. But, you said this aquarium has around a thousand? Let me ask you, what would this place do with that many volunteers?"

"There are all kinds of programs in place for our volunteers," Heather advised, as we walked by exhibit after exhibit. "Everyone wants to be a docent, but since those of our volunteers who have attained docent status don't want to give that up, we have quite a long waiting list in place."

"What is the difference between a docent and a volunteer?" Jillian wanted to know.

"Your basic volunteer is there to pretty much do whatever task has been assigned to them," Heather explained. "Clean tanks, feed animals, run errands, and so forth."

"You let volunteers feed the animals?" I asked. "Pardon me for saying so, but doesn't that sound like it could be dangerous for your animals?"

Heather laughed. "Well, you'd think so. However, assistant animal keeper has to be the second most sought-after status a volunteer strives for, with docent holding first place. Now, you asked about docents? Well, docents are those volunteers who don't get their hands dirty. They will guide people through exhibits. They'll talk to the public about their assigned species. They're the ones who typically speak for the aquarium when an actual staff member isn't present."

"I can only imagine the amount of rules and guidelines that must be in place for those people," Jillian surmised.

"Pages and pages," Heather agreed. "And, when a volunteer is promoted to docent status, they have a rigorous and thorough training program they have to pass."

"On top of agreeing to have a background check run on them," Jon added.

We were walking down a brightly lit hall, with rectangular openings placed every five feet. Each of the openings must have been a separate tank, since each window depicted a different species. Jon walked up to a concealed door, produced a ring full of color-coded keys, and selected a green-ringed key.

Opening the door, he guided all of us in. Having never been behind the scenes at any type of aquarium or zoo, I found the experience interesting. While on the other side of that door, every effort had been made to make it look as aesthetically pleasing as possible. On this side, however, nothing could've been further from the truth.

Pipes were running everywhere, from along the sides of the walls, to great big plastic mains running overhead. The window tanks, I could see, were just large 20-gallon aquariums, resting on wooden support platforms. A wooden boardwalk ran directly behind the tank, so that the attending aquarist would be physically higher than the tank itself, and could therefore observe the tank's occupants, perform maintenance, and so forth.

"That's really slick," I quietly observed, as I couldn't decide where to look first. Things were happening everywhere. "Here is someplace I wouldn't want to be after dark."

Heather laughed. "You sound like our swing keepers. We went through quite a few to find the two who trade off during the week. You'd think one of our exhibits featured Freddy Krueger."

"This place does make some unusual noises at night," Jon agreed, as he led us down the narrow walkway. "Here we are. Mind your step. If you'll follow me, I'll show you Mr. Carlton's office."

I held Jillian's hand as we carefully stepped down the narrow wooden steps, which returned us to floor-level. We followed Mary as she disappeared through an open doorway, which led into a small sitting room. Three other doors were visible; only one, however, was open. And, it just so happened to be the one Jon had stopped in front of, and was now staring aghast at what was visible through the open door.

The office had been ransacked!

FIVE

The following day started way too early for my liking. I mean, I was in the middle of La La Land, happily taking on the Empire, behind the controls of my X-Wing fighter, when an explosion occurred way too close to the nose of my fighter. I tried to bank around it, but suddenly, my controls were frozen. I pulled back on the control stick for all I was worth, yet my fighter sped on, oblivious to what I was trying to make it do. Then, as is the case with many of my dreams, the scene shifted, and suddenly, my X-Wing was headed straight for a body of water.

"Crap!" I swore. "Crap, crap, crap!"

I hit the water at what felt like light-speed, only I knew I was doomed. Water hit me square in the face, and just like that, my Star Wars adventure was over. Blinking profusely, and trying to rub the sleep out of my eyes, I suddenly became aware of two wet, furry bodies in bed with me. My brain literally couldn't process that. I'm sure a few circuits shorted out as I waited for my eyes to clear and I could see just what was going on.

There I was, in bed, with two damp corgis. Each of them, I might add, was trying to snuggle with me, while my adorable girlfriend laughed at me from the doorway.

"Sorry about that. I really did try to stop them before coming back here."

"No worries," I yawned, as I sat upright and looked at the two wriggling dogs on the bed. I should also mention that sand and dirt were everywhere. "Nice, guys. This is gonna take some explaining to the housekeepers."

"Zachary, you need to come see what we found!"

I focused a bleary eye on my girlfriend and gave her a smile, "Exactly how long have you been awake? I mean, what time is it now?"

"It's just after seven a.m.," Jillian told me.

"Feels a lot earlier," I decided.

"Hurry, get dressed! You need to see this."

Showered, shaved, and (mostly) presentable, I followed as she headed outside and—presumably —back to the water.

"Where's Harry and Julie?"

"They're not up yet."

"Have you always been this much of a morning person?" I asked.

She looked at me and gave me a million dollar smile, "Of course. You aren't?"

"Umm, I'm probably more of a night owl. But, the dogs don't typically let me sleep in anymore."

"That's why I let myself out and took Sherlock

and Watson with me," Jillian told me. "Anyway, I took the dogs for a walk. Sherlock wanted to go back to the water, so we headed toward McAbee Beach again. And, sure enough, the otters were back, just as playful as ever."

"That explains the wet dogs," I mused. "Wait. Watson was wet, too. Did she go in?"

"Almost immediately after Sherlock did, yes. I even think she's a better swimmer than Sherlock."

"I wouldn't have called that," I decided.

"Me, either. Did you know that otters are a part of the Mustelid family?"

"How much coffee have you had?"

"One or two cups. I forget. So, about the otters. They're in the Mustelid family!"

"And Mustelids are what, exactly?" I wanted to know.

"Weasels actually," Jillian answered. "Otters and weasels are related. I didn't know that. Did you know that? Anyway, I also found out a group of otters, floating together on the water, is called a raft. But, if you put those same otters on dry land, they'll then become a romp."

"A romp and raft," I slowly repeated.

"And otter nests are called holts."

"Did you watch a PBS special on otters?" I asked, amazed. "How have you become an otter expert all of a sudden?"

"I did wake up rather early," Jillian finally admitted. "I wanted to let you sleep in, so I started watching videos on my iPad. I was curious about otters, so I did some research. And that, unfortunately, must have awakened the dogs."

"It's okay," I assured her.

"Do you think the police have found any prints from Jack Carlton's office?" Jillian asked, as we left the hotel parking lot and headed toward the beach where we had seen those otters a few times.

"Well, Mary seemed to think they might be able to find a print or two. After all, according to her, typical ransacked crime scenes will have something to offer. There were just too many items in there that had been knocked over or touched. Plus, I overheard her telling someone, probably Officer Lewis, that she was planning on pulling in some additional officers to help process the scene."

"I just wish the most recent dive log would have still been there," Jillian said. "I mean, the older ones were there but, clearly, someone didn't want his most recent diving trips known. I'm with the director. I want to know where the last place Jack Carlton went diving was and who he went diving with. But, I think Mary was right. I think that record was what the thief was after."

"Now that I think about it," I mused, "wouldn't the trashed office suggest they couldn't find the most recent dive log?"

"Or else they were looking for something else, in addition to that dive log," Jillian suggested.

"The aquarium does have video surveillance," I recalled. "Jon said he and the security team were going to search the footage to see if there's any chance the perp who pulled it off was caught on tape. Hopefully, they'll be able to spot whether or not the perp was holding anything."

"I don't think they'll find anything," Jillian said. "Do you remember what Jon asked? He wanted to know how someone could have made it behind the scenes and been able to open the door leading into those three offices."

"He thinks it was an inside job," I recalled.

Jillian nodded. "Precisely. Look at the facts. Whoever did this clearly knew where the office was located. He must have access to keys, because there was no sign of forced entry. And, he knew which office was Jack Carlton's."

"They said Jack had tons of admirers there at the aquarium," I recalled. "There's gotta be someone who either didn't like him very much, or else was jealous of his popularity. It always happens."

I knew we were nearing the water, because first of all, I could hear the chirps and squeals the otters were making. But, the dead giveaway was how anxious my two dogs were in trying to rejoin their friends. Both of them morphed into their Clydesdale personas and forcefully pulled me to the water's edge.

Sure enough, the group of otters, er, make that the raft of otters, was still there, including the small youngster that had taken a liking to the dogs. The young otter, called a pup for all you otter aficionados, swam close, chirped and cooed, and then dove beneath the surface. Moments later, the pup was back, and he was still peering straight at the dogs.

"They want to play with them again," Jillian told me. "Should we?"

"They did okay the last time?" I warily asked.

Jillian nodded. "They did. There were no signs of aggression on either part."

"They're already wet. Go ahead. I've got my swim trunks on again, just in case."

"I remember," Jillian teased. "It was my idea. Look at Watson go! I hope the otters play with them again. It's what I wanted you to see. They are adorable together!"

I shook my head as I stared at the swimming corgis. And Watson? She was swimming like a pro! In fact ...

"She's swimming faster than Sherlock," I said, amazed, "and I don't think he likes that one bit!"

Watching the dogs play, Jillian and I sat back on the same rock we had sat upon before. While the dogs continued to play with the young otter, our attention drifted to the rest of the group, er, raft. I sighed. A raft of otters. It just doesn't roll off the tongue, does it?

"What's the matter?" Jillian asked, concerned. "Are you okay? Is your shoulder bothering you again?"

I automatically flexed my right shoulder and shook my head. "It's all right. I was actually thinking about the term 'raft.' It just doesn't sound right."

Jillian shrugged. "Well, I didn't come up with the term. Oh, Zachary, look! Do you see the otter closest to us? The one that just resurfaced? Do you see him? He's holding a clam in his front paws."

The otter in question was currently floating on its back and was rotating the clam this way and that, as though it was looking for a weak spot. Right about then, a rock was produced, and the otter began to bang the rock against the shell. After a few moments, the shell broke, and the otter enjoyed its meal.

"I wonder where the rock came from," I pondered. "He was holding that clam before. If I didn't know any better, then I'd say he pulled that rock out of thin air."

"I'm so glad you asked," Jillian exclaimed. "Under the otter's front legs is a loose pouch of skin. They can store excess food and typically, a small rock, with which to help them break open clams and crabs."

"A small pouch, huh?"

"Usually under their left front paw."

"You're something, do you know that?"

"I was bored this morning. Plus, the documentary was interesting. I'm just surprised I didn't wake you up. It was rather loud."

"I've been known to sleep through WWIII," I advised, with a chuckle.

A glint of light caught my eye. Looking out at the otters, I could see that the young otter, finished playing with the dogs, had now acquired his own meal, a small crab, and was busy trying to break open the crustacean's shell with his own rock. The dogs had returned to shore, and were both stretched out in the sand, watching the otters.

"I'm glad we brought their shampoo along," I mused. "We're gonna be needing it before I allow them back on the bed."

Another glint of light caught my eye. I looked back at the young otter, but this time, my attention was drawn to the otter's weapon of choice, namely his rock. Only, bits of his rock were reflecting light! How was that possible? Unless ... unless it was some type of metal?

"Do you see that?" I asked, as I pointed at Sherlock's pal, the otter pup. "I think the rock that otter is using has some type of metal on it."

"I've seen it, too," Jillian confirmed, as she rose to her feet. She shaded her eyes and studied the floating otter. "From this distance, it does look like a rock, only ... Zachary? Does that look like a coin of some sort to you?"

"It looks too big to be a coin," I decided. "I guess it could be a medallion? Maybe a pendant? I'm not sure."

"I wish I knew what it was," Jillian wistfully said.

At that moment, both dogs bolted back into the water, startling the otters. The entire group of them—yeah, that's right, I'm calling 'em group, and not raft—disappeared underwater. The young otter was one of them, only we both noticed the otter had dropped his *rock* before swimming away.

"Now's our chance!" Jillian excitedly told me.

"Now's our chance for what?" I cautiously asked.

My girlfriend pointed out at the water.

"You're wearing swim trunks. We wanted to see what the otter was holding, and we both saw him drop it. What do you think? Can you find it?"

"Out there??" I exclaimed, as I pointed a finger at the waves gently lapping at the shore. "Can we say, needle in a haystack?"

"You should look for it."

"Seriously?"

"Yes. I've seen you get wet before. Your clothes always seem to dry in record time. I've never been able to figure that out."

Not knowing how to respond to that, I shrugged helplessly.

"Would you try looking?" Jillian pleaded. "For me?"

"We have no idea how deep that is," I protested.

Jillian batted her eyes at me. I sighed. Women should not be allowed to pull out their Bambi eyes on the opposite sex. How are we ever supposed to say no?

"Thank you, Zachary," Jillian said, as I grudgingly stripped off my shirt.

I waded into the water and stifled a curse. Holy freakin' hell, was that water cold. The sun may have been out, and it might have been a balmy 70 degrees or so, but in the water? It felt as though I'd see a passing iceberg at any moment.

"A little more to your right," Jillian called from shore. "A little more. Okay, that's perfect. Now, head out to sea."

"The things I do for love," I sputtered, as I felt the ground drop away from under my feet. That, of course, meant I was now treading water. I meant what I said earlier. I'd sink like a stone if I stopped moving, which means the simple act of keeping my head above water was a chore for me.

"It's not far, Zachary. Good, you're almost there. There! That's perfect! The otter was right where you are!"

Here we go, I silently mused. I took a deep breath and dipped below the surface.

I'm going to pause here a moment and remind you, the reader, about something. You heard me mention that the temperature of the water felt like it was freezing? Well, that was nothing to what I was experiencing now. I had always heard that your head will put off a lot of heat. Take that heat source and dip it in ice water, and you'll find that you're having a most unpleasant day.

The cold water hit me like a brutal slap in the face. Trying to find the otter's rock dropped to a very low ranking on the Totem Pole of Priorities. What was number one? Getting myself out of the water just as soon as possible. Based on the headache that had just erupted with the force of a freight train, I knew I wouldn't be able to stay in the water for too much longer, let alone stay underwater. So, if I had any hope of finding whatever the otter had been holding, it had better be within the next five minutes.

Actually, it took me eight.

Holding the object in my hand victoriously above my head as I surfaced, I let out a loud whoop and hurriedly swam for shore.

"You found it!" Jillian exclaimed.

"Y-y-you s-s-sound s-surprised," I said, through chattering teeth. I stared at the rock I was holding with trembling hands and grinned. "L-l-look! Y-y-you're r-right. Th-there's s-s-something in th-this r-rock."

Concerned, Jillian pulled the metallic rock from my hand and laid a hand on my arm. Her eyes opened wide.

"I had no idea the water was so cold. You're freezing!"

"Y-y-you d-d-don't s-s-say."

"Come on. Let's go back to the hotel and get you warmed up."

There definitely wouldn't be any arguments from me. As I have gone on record as saying before, I'm frequently wrong. In this case, I was in a full-on raging argument less than fifteen minutes later. What was it about? Well, Jillian had decreed that I needed a hot beverage to help warm me up from the inside. She had determined—correctly, I might add—that my core temp had dropped significantly while I was in the water. So, she took it upon herself to make something for me to drink.

However ...

In a hotel room, what does a person typically find when they want to make a hot beverage? Coffee. And there are tea bags, for those who prefer it. As for me? I'm not a hot beverage type of guy, but Jillian wouldn't hear it. She ignored my complaints and presented me with a steaming cup of coffee and a steeping mug of tea.

"Pick one. I don't care which it is, but you're drinking one."

"I ... I'll b-be f-fine. J-just g-give me a f-few minutes t-to w-warm up."

"It's been nearly half an hour, and you're still chattering. Which is it going to be?"

I made the mistake of looking at my two choices and adopting a defiant stance. Less than thirty seconds later, I had the mug of tea in my hand, appreciating the warmth it was returning to my fingers, while trying to choke down the bile liquid that tasted like flowers.

"Stop making that face. Admit it. You're feeling better."

"I don't know how I'm gonna get this taste out of my mouth."

"Uh huh."

"What?" I asked, growing defensive.

"Your teeth aren't chattering, and you're no longer shivering. I'd say the tea is working."

"Can I stop drinking it?"

"Is it gone?"

"No."

"There's your answer."

I sighed, willed my taste buds to not revolt, and downed as much of the tea as I could. Chamomile. *Blech.*

"If I knew you'd drink hot soda, then I would have given that a try," Jillian said a few minutes later, as she took the empty mug from me. "I'm sorry I did that to you."

"You're looking out for me. Believe it or not, I appreciate it. However ..."

"... you still hate tea," Jillian guessed, as she gave me a relieved smile.

"With the fiery passion of a hundred suns."

An hour later, I felt well enough to take another shower, but not until I gave both dogs a bath. Only then, did I feel like I was myself again. Important safety note: If you plan on going into the waters off the California Coast, or Oregon for that matter, then you had better plan on wearing a wetsuit. Hypothermia is no laughing matter.

Hanging my damp clothes out to dry on the handy-dandy clothes line thingamajig most hotel showers have, I returned to the room to see Jillian sitting at the desk. She held the metallic object in her hands and was peering closely at it, no doubt attempting to determine the source of the metal we noticed earlier.

Noticing the corgis were leaving damp splotches on the bedspread, I grabbed several extra towels I had found in a cabinet and decided to try and dry them off as much as I could. One wet corgi + one determined daddy with a towel = one sassy dog who avoided me like the plague. Throw a second dog into the mix, and I had my hands full. I really don't know what I was concerned about. Sherlock and Watson were streaking around the room at Mach 1. All I had to do was to keep it up, and the dogs would air-dry themselves. That is, until, somehow, the tables were turned and suddenly, the towel morphed into the Mortal Enemy of all Corgis and both dogs were attacking it. Sherlock managed to yank the towel out of my hands and, triumphantly, jumped up onto the bed and proceeded to start chewing on it.

"Give that back," I ordered. "If you don't knock it off, then this hotel is gonna charge us for those things. You want to chew on something? Here. I have something for you."

I pulled out the honest-to-goodness diaper bag I had created for the dogs, and retrieved a bag full of their favorite chew toys. Mollified, both dogs settled down onto the bed and tore into their rawhide bones. Being close to the desk, I pulled up a chair next to the bed and positioned myself next to Jillian.

"Found anything out yet?"

Jillian nodded. "Some. I was able to remove this barnacle and now we've got more of the surface uncovered. Do you see this here? And over here? I can just make out some lettering. That looks like an X, and this over here looks like ANI. What do you think that means?"

"It's gotta be some type of medallion," I deduced. "Look at the size of it. I don't think it could be a coin."

"American Silver dollars are about this size," Jillian argued.

"You think this is the same size as an Eisenhower dollar coin?" I asked.

Jillian handed me the item so that I could judge for myself.

"No, I'd say this is bigger. I mean, look at the overall shape of this thing. I'd say it's clear that there's something buried within this ... this ... whatever this crusty stuff is. But I don't think it's a coin. It's a medallion."

"Coin," Jillian insisted.

"Medallion," I grinned.

"And we have an impasse," Jillian giggled. "Very well. We need to see if we can figure out what this is. Do you think there's anyone in town we can go to?"

"Besides our pal, Chet?"

Jillian nodded. "He'd be a great place to start. Come on. Let's go pay him a visit."

* * *

"Welcome back!" Chet exclaimed, as he held the door open for us. "I was hoping to hear from you two again, but I didn't think it'd be this soon. You said on the phone that you had found something? Something in the water? Well, curiosity kills. May I see it?"

Jillian produced the young otter's rock and held it out.

"Where did you find this again?" Chet asked, as he took the object and studied it.

"An otter was using it to break clams open," Jillian answered. "Right off of Cannery Row, almost adjacent to the aquarium."

"I know the area you mean," Chet said, as he ushered us inside his home. He brought us deeper inside his mansion and eventually stopped outside a stainless steel door. Chet saw my quizzical look and smiled. "It looks out of place, I know, but considering what's on the other side of this door, I felt it appropriate."

"And what, exactly, is on the other side?" I cautiously asked.

In answer to my question, Chet opened the door, revealing a well-equipped mini lab, complete with microscopes, computers, work tables, and shelves of books. Racks of small tools were hanging on pegs in neat rows above the closest work table. Chet rolled an adjustable stool over to the table, sat, and selected a few tools from his rack.

"I thought you were just a coin collector," I said, amazed at the equipment in the room.

"One doesn't live in Monterey without having a love of the water," Chet explained. He was now wearing a headband magnifier and was examining the mysterious object. "I've been a certified diver practically all my life. You never know what you may find, and if you do find something, it's always helpful to be able to figure out what it is."

"Have you ever found any coins out there?" Jillian asked.

Chet nodded. "Several, actually. They really weren't worth too much. But, that pales in comparison to the excitement of finding something that could be anything. I can see some lettering here."

"We saw it, too," I confirmed. "Any idea what it says?"

"Let's see if we can get this cleaned up a bit."

A noise reminiscent of a dentist's drill suddenly started up. It reminded me way too much of my last dental visit, so I slapped both hands over my ears. Watson whined, but Sherlock gave the strange noise the full-on head tilt.

"My, my, my. What have we here?"

Jillian and I crowded close to Chet to see what he was doing. In this case, a large piece of the 'rock' had flaked away, revealing more tantalizing bits of metal underneath. Now, besides some lettering, we could see some shapes start to materialize.

"This looks like some type of building here," Chet explained, as he rinsed the coin in distilled water. "And here? Hmm, it looks like another building."

"Is it a medallion?" I hopefully asked.

"Definitely a coin," Chet answered.

"Damn," I swore.

"Told you," Jillian teased. "Is there anything on the reverse side?"

Chet flipped the coin over and touched the tip of his micro drill to the side. The god-awful, high-pitched whine filled my ears again, and just like that, another large flake fell off the coin. Once more, Chet dunked the coin in the tub of distilled water and then dried it off. His eyes narrowed as he studied the newly revealed picture.

"What is that stuff that's flaking off like that?" I asked.

"Probably lime deposits," Chet said, as he picked up his drill and removed a few other pieces of gray deposits. "Hmm, do you see this here? It looks like arches, does it not?"

I shrugged. "I'll give you that. Arches on a coin. What does that mean?"

Chet's eyes widened and he stifled a curse.

"No. It cannot be."

"What?" I demanded. "You recognize this, don't you? Well, what is it?"

"Just a moment," Chet pleaded. "I need to know for sure. If you'll allow me?" He held up his tiny drill and waggled it.

Jillian and I shared a look with each other. She nodded.

"Of course."

Chet, exhibiting a precision to his work that wasn't there a few moments ago, carefully removed more of the mineral deposits. Our new friend spent the next fifteen minutes in complete silence as he meticulously worked on extricating the coin from the rock. Every few minutes or so, he'd hold the coin with a pair of tongs and then would dip it in a second bin, followed almost immediately by the first. I could only assume he was submerging it in some type of acid, or maybe cleaning solution, and then quickly rinsing it off.

"I'll be darned," Chet finally said. He pulled his magnifier off his head and stretched his back. Turning to the two of us, he held the coin up with his tongs. "You asked me if I recognized it, right?"

Jillian nodded.

"The answer to that is yes, I do. Why? Well, because this is my coin. My friends, this is the coin I asked you to recover for me!"

SIX

You're sure?" I asked, trying hard to keep the skeptical tone out of my voice. "This is your coin? I mean, come on. What are the odds of that?"

We were now sitting in Chet's study, which was, by my reckoning, three hallways and two rooms over from his lab. Our coin-collecting friend sat back in his armchair and studied the former rock in his gloved hand. He reached for his glass of wine and took a healthy drink. Jillian and I automatically reached for the beer bottles our host had obligingly offered to us and followed suit. For me, it might have been more of a guzzle.

"This is a 1721 Spanish Silver 2 Reales Piece of 8 coin. The bit of lettering you saw earlier, the X and the ANI you told me about, was just a few of the letters encircling the coin. You can see it now reads, 1721 HISPANIARUM REX. Those buildings we saw? They were castles, located in the upper left quadrant and the lower right. And in the upper right and lower left? You can see that they are lions."

"Is there any writing on the other side?" I wanted to know.

Chet nodded and turned the coin over. He tapped the letters that curved around the outside of the coin.

"Philipus V."

"And that's a person," I guessed.

"King Philip the Fifth," Chet confirmed. "He ruled from 1716-1740. This particular coin was placed in general circulation. Do you see the crowned M?"

"Where?" Jillian asked, as she leaned close.

"Here," Chet said, tapping the area near the V of King Philip's name. "That's Madrid's mint mark."

"You clearly know your coins," Jillian said. "I, er, am glad we could return it to you."

"I am absolutely astounded to have this sitting in my hand, after all this time," Chet was saying, as he stared lovingly at the silver coin sitting in his palm. "Especially since I only officially asked for your help yesterday. I take my hat off to you, my friends, and your wonderful dogs. I will telephone the captain immediately and express my thanks."

Bidding goodbye to our new friend, the four of us headed back to town, via another ridesharing app. Telephoning ahead, we learned that Harry and Julie were now awake and arranged to meet them at a local restaurant for a bite to eat. Since this place didn't have an outside terrace, the dogs would have to stay confined in the room. However, since both corgis had been swimming in the ocean earlier, then given baths, and then were given two car rides, I didn't think we were going to have a problem. A quick look back as we exited the room confirmed that Sherlock was now on his back, with all four paws in the air, and Watson was lying next to him. They were out cold.

"Do you really mean it?" Harry asked, as soon as we sat down next to them and ordered some drinks. "We're really getting the rooms for free?"

"We haven't heard anything yet from the police department," Jillian cautioned. "I honestly wouldn't plan on not paying your bill until the clerk at the front desk says the bill has been paid in full. It's not worth it. I mean, we are on vacation, after all."

"Hey, a bet's a bet," Harry argued.

"Tell me about that coin," Julie implored. "I can't believe you found it so quickly! That's awesome, you two!"

"We didn't find it," I corrected. "Sherlock did. In fact, he's been pulling us to the water ever since we gave the keys to the hotel's valet. That dog is something else. I just don't buy it, though."

"What?" Harry wanted to know. "What don't you buy?"

At that time, the waitress appeared and took our order. It was 10:30 a.m., and still technically breakfast, but I was tempted to order a burger. Jillian saw me looking at the lunch side of the menu and shook her head. She knew I loved my burgers, but she also knew that, thanks to my last doctor's appointment, my cholesterol was on the higher side. His recommendation? Cut out red meat. Eat more green vegetables. The quack. Getting old sucks.

We placed our orders, with me ordering a heart-healthy egg white omelet with added avocado slices. I waited for the waitress to wander off before I answered Harry's question.

"Sherlock is good," I slowly began. "Both dogs are. But come on, don't you think it's a little convenient that we were asked to locate a stolen coin, only to discover it in the hands of… er, in the paws of a local otter? And this, happening on the day after we were asked to look for it?"

"They're your dogs," Harry reminded me. "You've told us many times how amazing they are at finding stuff. Think about it, man. This is just another occasion where the dogs find something that no one else could have. I mean, think back to that ugly glass tiger."

"Yeah, I know."

"Or the missing Egyptian pendant," Jillian added.

"Or the thief who was stealing all the Christmas presents?" Julie reminded me.

"This list goes on and on, man," Harry pointed out.

"What's your point?" I asked. "I know all about the cases those two dogs have solved. I mean, I was there, remember?"

"The point we're trying to make," my girlfriend soothingly explained, "is that this is just another example of how gifted the dogs are. I cannot explain how they can do what they do. You can't. Neither can Harry, and he's the professional."

"I am," Harry jovially confirmed.

Julie smacked him on the arm, but playfully so, I noted.

"You're saying I need to let this one go and just reward them with a box of Scooby Snacks? Is that it?"

"They just saved us each over $700," Harry reminded me. "Don't be a cheapskate. Get 'em each a case."

"Hardy ha ha."

We had our breakfasts, and I ate my tasteless omelet. The one thing I did enjoy, strangely enough, was the addition of the avocado slices. Growing up, I avoided any food that had a hint of avocado, seeing how they were green. Only now, I think I had inadvertently been cheating myself. That part of my breakfast was good.

Just as I was finishing up my glass of juice, my cell rang. A quick check of the display had me grinning. It was the local police department.

"Hello?"

"Zack? It's Mary."

"Hi, Mary. What's up?"

"We just received the autopsy report on Jack Carlton."

"I thought for certain you were going to say something about that coin," I confessed. I let out a chuckle. "All right, hit me with your best. Did the autopsy find anything useful?"

"First, let me congratulate you guys. Chet Mayberry called the captain personally, and extolled your dogs' skills. He couldn't be more thrilled about the return of his coin. That is one happy numismatist."

"That's one happy what?"

"Numismatist. It's the technical name for a coin collector or coin enthusiast."

"You learn something new each day. Numismatist. Got it. I'm following along now. He called the captain? Do you have any idea what the captain said?"

"He's already contacted your hotel. Your bill has been paid, and he sends his thanks."

"I have a friend here who will be thrilled to death to hear that."

Overhearing, Harry let out a whoop of joy as he correctly guessed what I was talking about.

"With regards to Jack Carlton's death, the cause of death has been confirmed: drowning. Sea water was found in his lungs."

"That isn't too surprising," I decided. "It sounds like an open and shut case. I mean, he was a diver, and we found him face down in the water."

"But ... tetrodotoxin was also found in his system."

"Tetris-what?" I asked, as my tongue tripped over the unfamiliar word.

"Tetrodotoxin," Mary carefully repeated. "It's

an incredibly dangerous neurotoxin."

"A dangerous neurotoxin," I repeated, for Jillian's benefit. "That sounds really bad."

"Tetrodotoxin poisoning messes with the signals your nerves send to your muscles. In essence, it causes paralysis. Too much can be fatal."

"So, he died from this Tetris poison?"

"Tetrodotoxin," Mary repeated, for the fourth time. "And no. Cause of death has already been established: drowning. The seawater in his lungs confirmed that."

"Then, how did the ..." I paused as I tried to repeat the name of the poison in my head. Nope. Couldn't do it. "... poison get into his system? Was it something he ate? Or ingested?"

"No, not with this stuff. It's incredibly fast acting. The deceased would have had to come into contact with it while he was out in the water."

"Oh, I get it. He got stung by a jellyfish or something like that?"

"I wondered the same thing, too," Mary admitted. "The answer is, no. While the sting of a jellyfish can be painful, and there are those that can be fatal, the most well-known source of tetrodotoxin would be a certain species of puffer fish. There are also, I've recently learned, certain tropical frogs, newts, crabs, starfish, and even octopuses that have it. I don't understand the basics of it yet, but I've put in a few calls to some friends of mine. I hope to know more later."

"Well, you just described all kinds of sea life," I

said. "Jack Carlton was a world-famous diver, and he worked in an aquarium. He must have come into contact with it at some point in time."

"Mr. Anderson, you're not hearing me. Once the tetrodotoxin has been introduced into your system, the symptoms can appear anywhere from just a few minutes to several hours. It all depends on how much neurotoxin was introduced into the bloodstream, and where it came from."

"Could he have built up an immunity to this stuff? You know, like how Westley built up his resistance to iocane?"

"*The Princess Bride*. Ah, I loved that movie. You have great tastes in movies, Mr. Anderson. But no, this stuff is way too dangerous to fiddle around with. Any knowledgeable diver would steer clear of any animal that carried it."

"Then he had to have encountered something out in the water," I deduced.

"That's what I think, too," Mary admitted. "The problem with that logic is, everything we're aware of that can carry tetrodotoxin lives in tropical waters. There's nothing native to this area."

"For the sake of argument, let's say Jack Carlton managed to find something out there that carried this tetrodotoxin crap," I began, "how much ..."

"Tetro..." Mary interrupted. "You were close on that one."

"Yeah, thanks. Okay, tetrodotoxin. How much of that stuff was in the victim's system?"

"I don't know."

"You have the autopsy reports," I reminded the Monterey cop. "Doesn't it say how much of the neurotoxin was present?"

"That's a good point. Let me see. Here it is. 3.7 milligrams."

"That's ... that's a really low amount, isn't it?"

"Incredibly so. But, listen to this. The lab technician made some notes. He said that it only takes 1-2 milligrams to kill an adult."

"How does that help us?"

"It means Jack Carlton was murdered."

I terminated the call after I thanked Mary for the information. My mind was spinning. Jack Carlton was murdered? And some powerful neurotoxin was found in his blood? Was that why a skilled diver was found face down in the water? That toxin paralyzed him and he drowned? What a horrible way to die!

"What's going on?" Jillian asked, as I sat back in my chair and polished off my soda.

Yeah, I know. Omelets and sodas. You'd think it'd be a terrible mix, but it works for me. Especially if I have to choke down an egg white omelet.

"That was Mary, from the police department. The autopsy came in for the dead diver we found."

"And?" Harry prompted.

"Cause of death is still drowning," I relayed, which caused my three companions to nod their heads knowingly, "only there's a twist involved. Some neurotoxin was also found in his blood."

"The Tetris toxin?" Jillian teased.

"Hey, it's a long word," I argued. "Tetrodotoxin. There, I finally got it right, only Mary's not here. Oh, well."

"Tetrodotoxin," Harry solemnly repeated. "I've heard of that stuff, man. You don't screw around with it."

"How have you heard of it?" I wanted to know. "Did you take a class on toxins?"

"Kinda," Harry said, nodding. "Quite a few of our classes did, actually. They focused on what we can do to keep the patient alive, and what not to give the patient to make them dead."

I had been taking a drink from my soda when I snorted with amusement. Yep, there was the Harry I knew. His acerbic wit never grew old. And that, my friends, is called sarcasm.

"Jerk," I grumbled.

Jillian giggled and swatted my arm.

"I only ever saw it in use on tree frogs," Harry admitted. "You can find some shitty things out in the tropics, bro."

"Watch your language, Harrison," Julie scolded.

"Sorry, Jillian," Harry apologized.

Jillian nodded and waved a dismissive hand.

"Well, what should we do now?" Julie asked.

"We haven't been asked to do anything with regards to the murder," I said, shrugging. "However, I would like to take care of something that's bothering me, and it requires doing a little research. However, this is your vacation, too, so if you don't want to tag along, I'll understand."

"What's on your mind?" Jillian wanted to know.

"That coin," I answered. "I just don't buy the odds. Yes, the dogs found it, and they're amazing. I know it. You guys know it. I'm pretty sure they know it, too. Only ..."

"... it doesn't feel right," Jillian finished for me.

I grinned. "Exactly."

"What do you want to do?" my girlfriend asked.

"I want to find out more about that coin."

"You want to go back to the coin dude's place?" Harry asked.

"Not particularly," I admitted. "There's gotta be other research options at our disposal."

"This is Monterey," Jillian reminded us. "It's known for its diving. I'm sure we're not the only people who have ever found a strange coin. I'll bet the local library has something to offer."

"A library?" Harry whined. "Oh, man. Not my idea of fun, bro."

"And what do you want to do that's so important?" Julie asked, as she turned to her husband.

"Can't we hit a bar or something? I could use a ..."

My friend trailed off as he noticed the disapproving frown his wife was giving him. About to scowl, I caught Harry's eye and then patted my own belly. Harry groaned.

"You're on a diet now," Julie reminded him. "If

you're looking for something to do, well, we could go snorkeling. That'd be fun, wouldn't it?"

"That water is too cold for snorkeling, Jules," Harry said, frowning. "We'd need the proper gear."

"If you want, you could swing by the hotel and take the dogs out," I suggested. "I would appreciate it and so would they, I'm sure."

"We'll take care of it," Julie assured us. "Come on, Harrison."

"I get Sherlock this time," I heard Harry's voice say, as our two friends walked away.

Thirty minutes later, we had found the Monterey Public Library. Jillian promptly walked to the closest computer terminal and started tapping in commands.

"All right. I'm logged in, and I've got a search engine open. Now, what can you remember about that coin?" Jillian asked.

"It was Spanish," I immediately said. "The year stamped on the coin was 1721. Oh, and something about reales. Chet said it was a two reales coin."

I heard Jillian tapping on the keyboard as I relayed what I could remember. After a few moments, a list of results appeared on the screen. Jillian scrolled through a few before stopping at a familiar coin.

"That's it," I confirmed. "Do you see the castles in the top left and bottom right?"

"And the lions in the other two quadrants," Jillian added, as she clicked on the image of the coin. "It says here it was minted for King Phillip V. It's not necessarily a rare coin, as people have been buying and selling them at auction for years."

"What's it worth?" I wanted to know.

"Depends on the quality," Jillian told me.

She entered in the search parameters at an auction website and sat back so I could see the results.

"Here's one for $100. There's one for $500, but there aren't any bids. Yeah, I see what you mean. Some of the coins have sharp details. Others look as though they've been attacked by a sander."

"Those are probably the coins that have been found underwater," Jillian theorized.

"Makes sense."

"They're attributed to a lot of shipwrecks," Jillian added, several minutes later.

"Oh? Which ones?"

"There are too many to name. Spain transported a lot of treasure during the years this particular coin was in circulation. It says here that a typical Spanish galleon could have been loaded with two million of these coins, weighing close to 60 tons. No wonder there were so many pirate ships during that time period. That must have been too tempting of a target to pass up. It must be why Pieces of Eight and doubloons have been found on the beaches of all the Americas."

"That coin could have been part of a real-life pirate treasure horde," I mused. "Incredible."

"Zachary, you're grinning like a schoolboy who has just been let out for the summer. What is it with men and pirate treasure?"

Before I could answer that, my cell rang. I checked the display and saw that another local Monterey number was calling, only this time, it wasn't Mary, and I'm pretty sure it wasn't Chet, the coin guy. Who else did I know in town?

"Hello?"

"Hi," a woman's voice hesitantly said. "Um, is this Zachary Anderson?"

"Well, you know me. Do I know you?"

"Actually, yes, you do. We met the other day. I'm Sherry. Sherry VanZanten. We, uh, met not long after Jack Carlton's body had been discovered."

"The woman hiding in the bushes," I recalled.

"I wasn't hiding!" Sherry protested. "Jeez, would you give a girl a break? You sound just like the police."

"How did you get my number, Sherry?" I wanted to know. "We didn't exchange contact information."

"I'm sorry. I looked you up online."

"My cell phone isn't listed online," I told the girl. "Would you care to try again?"

"All right! I'm sorry! I asked a friend at the police department to pass me your number."

"See? Now that I can believe. Why have you called me, Sherry? Is there something I can do for you?"

"My friend says that you're a police consultant in Oregon. Is that correct?"

"I hold several job titles. Police consultant is

one of them. Why do you ask? If you have need of the police, then I would suggest you talk to an actual police officer, and that isn't me, I'm sorry to say."

"I need your help. I want you to find out who did this to Jack."

"You said you were one of Jack's volunteers, right?"

"What of it?"

"Well, I need to know something. Did Jack do a lot of diving in Monterey?"

"He liked looking for wrecks. Why do you ask?"

"Because I want to know. I want to know where he was diving and who he was diving with. Did you know his most recent dive log is missing?"

"Why would you think I had something to do with that?"

"I didn't say that you did. You just assumed I did. Man alive, why do you keep throwing questions back at me whenever I ask you one? If I didn't know any better, then I'd say you're hiding something, Sherry. What ..."

The line went dead.

"Is everything okay?" Jillian asked, as she looked over at me. "I heard you say the name Sherry. Wasn't that the name of the woman who was found hiding in the bushes?"

"One and the same," I confirmed.

"What did she want?"

"Somehow, she found out I am a police consultant and wanted me and the dogs to find out what happened to Jack."

"Did she call him by his full name or did she refer to him by his first name?"

I thought back to Sherry's request.

"First name only. Is that important?"

"She totally had a thing for him," Jillian deduced. "If it wasn't intimate, then she wanted it to be."

"What's that supposed to mean?" I asked.

"She had a crush on him."

"Do you think she was stalking him?"

"Well, if she was, then she'd be the perfect person to talk to. Maybe she knew of someone who wanted Jack Carlton out of the picture."

"Like a rival," I guessed.

"Or enemy," Jillian added. "Same thing, I guess."

"Do you know what else she said?" I asked, as I recalled another part of Sherry's cryptic conversation. "I asked her if she knew whether or not Jack Carlton liked to dive in Monterey. Sherry informed me that he liked looking for wrecks, and almost immediately afterward, she went on the defensive. Started asking questions every time I did. I think she was moments away from panicking, which was why she hung up on me."

Jillian frowned. "She hung up on you? That's rude. I don't care who you are, you just don't do that to people. Hmm. Zachary, why do you suddenly look so excited?"

I pointed back at the screen, which still showed pictures of the old Spanish coins.

"Don't you get it? I think Jack Carlton was looking for sunken treasure ships, and that coin confirms it!"

SEVEN

Does that make any sense to you?" Jillian asked later. "Think about it. If what you say is true, and that poor, unfortunate scuba diver was searching for sunken treasure, then how did Chet's stolen coin end up in the water? Are we to believe that a thief broke into Chet's home, somehow managed to get around his security system, steal only that one coin ..."

"... and pass up others that are more valuable," I glumly added.

"Yes. He passed up the more valuable coins, then took the one coin he did steal down to the water and gave it to an otter?"

I shrugged and shook my head. I didn't have a response to that.

"And," Jillian continued, "didn't that coin look like it had been in the water for a long time?"

I began nodding. "I'll give you that one. I've been wondering about that myself."

"Still think all of this makes sense?" Jillian challenged.

"When you say it like that, it might sound a little silly," I said, chuckling. "All right. Let's just toss that theory out the window, shall we?"

Jillian giggled, and then pointed west, toward the water. We could see Harry and Julie, walking hand in hand along the water, each holding one of the corgi's leashes. People were coming up to them left and right and—presumably—asking if they could pet the dogs, because both dogs kept rolling onto their backs to get their belly rubs.

"Those two," I groaned, as I heard Jillian laugh. "There's not one shred of dignity between either of them. Look at 'em. They're loving the attention."

Sherlock caught sight of me as we stepped down from the boardwalk onto the sandy beach. He yipped excitedly at us, as though he was inviting us to tag along with him.

"Exactly who owns who here?" I quietly asked, as we approached the dogs.

"They own you, of course," Jillian answered. "Well hello, pretty boy. Are you and Watson enjoying the day?"

"Your dogs have a lot of admirers, man," Harry announced. "Festus doesn't get near the attention that these two get."

Festus was Harry's Australian Shepherd. I always thought corgis had to be the most energetic dog I have ever encountered. Nope. Harry's dog wins that contest, hands down. The last time the four of us went over to his place, Festus ran laps around Sherlock and Watson the entire time we were there, which had to have been two or three hours.

"Where should we go?" Julie asked, as she handed Watson's leash to Jillian. I took Sherlock's and, together, the six of us headed back toward town. "What would you guys say about visiting Old Fisherman's Wharf?"

"What is it?" I wanted to know. "A restaurant?"

Julie handed me a pamphlet, simply entitled, Things to do in Old Fisherman's Wharf. First on the list was to enjoy a simple stroll down the historic wharf and check out the authentic seafood restaurants. We could also arrange to go whale watching, judging by the numerous boats lined up on the water's edge. Continuing, I read that Old Fisherman's Wharf was also the place to be if you wanted to purchase fine jewelry or ocean-themed keepsakes or ... Now, this next entry definitely caught my attention: candy stores.

Now, you may—or may not—know that I have a sweet tooth. That's not to say I had to have a piece of candy in my mouth during all hours of the day. However, if a tourist pamphlet recommends stopping by a shop that specializes in salt water taffy, then who am I to go against the local tourism board?

Right about then, my nose reported in that we were in the vicinity of one of these specialty stores.

"That smells heavenly," Jillian announced, as she drew to a stop. "Do you smell that? I swear its molten chocolate."

"You had me at *molten*," Julie said, laughing. "Come on, Harrison. We need to find whatever store is making that heavenly smell."

"It does smell good," Harry admitted.

"It's over there," I said, as I shaded my eyes and pointed across the street. "I see the word Carousel on the sign. Plus, you can see the steady stream of people going in and out of that store."

Harry and Julie hurried ahead, intent on entering the store first. I also noticed that they had been walking while holding hands together.

"I haven't seen them do that in a while," Jillian told me, in a quiet voice.

"It's nice to see," I agreed.

"What did you end up saying to Harry to get him to behave? I take it you've been giving him pointers."

"I told him he needs to learn the definition of a word: compromise. Be willing to bend on things she wants to do, and he'd be surprised on how much she'd be willing to return the favor. So far, it seems to be working. You've been talking to Julie, too, haven't you?"

Jillian nodded. "Guilty as charged."

I nodded my head toward Julie, who had just disappeared inside the candy store.

"Hey, we're good."

Taking my hand, Jillian led me into the shop. Harry, stating he didn't want to be tempted by all the sugary goodies inside the store, especially the melted chocolate, offered to wait outside with the dogs. While yes, I could definitely smell melted chocolate, and I knew that's what Jillian wanted to find, I was more intent on finding (and purchasing) some fresh taffy. My girlfriend, I had learned a while ago, loved chocolate turtles. What are they? In case you didn't know, they're candy made with pecans and caramel, covered in chocolate. Then they're shaped to loosely resemble a turtle.

And no, no actual turtles were harmed in the making of this highly sought-after candy.

As for me, as I mentioned earlier, I love salt water taffy. I enjoy more of the fruity candy than the chocolate variety. Oh, don't get me wrong, I'll certainly choke down a piece of chocolate every now and then. But, I can certainly go without it for extended periods of time. As for Jillian? Let's just say I have around a dozen different candy bars hidden in my fridge, with stashes of various goodies in a few other random spots, too.

You never know when your significant other will have a chocolate craving. Trust me, late night runs to the convenience store are never fun.

Arms loaded with goodies, and me munching on a small bag of candy-corn flavored taffy, we exited the candy store and followed the flow of foot traffic north. From what I could see, next up was some type of ocean-inspired gift shop. Jillian and I combined our bags and, with me holding the large bag in one hand and holding the door open with the other, we entered the store. Since there wasn't any food offered for sale in this shop, the dogs were allowed in.

I tried to focus on the various trinkets as I followed Jillian around the store, but my mind kept jumping over to the unfortunate Jack Carlton. Could he have been searching for treasure? If so, who was his dive partner? Where had he been diving? Couldn't it have been somewhere close to where I had originally spotted him?

I felt a tap on my arm. Looking up, I saw Jillian studying my face, with a concerned expression on hers.

"Are you all right? Are you not having a good time? We can go somewhere else, if you'd like."

I shook my head. "It's not that. My mind keeps drifting over to Jack Carlton. While possible, experienced divers simply don't go in the water alone. Plus, where was he diving? That Sherry girl said he frequently dived the area."

"We really need that missing dive log," Jillian said, as she moved to a table filled with folded shirts. "I don't know if we'll ever really know what he was up to without them."

A thought suddenly occurred.

"What do you think the chances are that Jack Carlton stole Chet's coin?"

Jillian shrugged. "I doubt it. From the sounds of it, he was loaded. If he really wanted one of those coins, he could have just bought one. Or two. Or even a hundred."

"True," I reluctantly agreed. "Do you even think the two events are related?"

"What, finding the dead diver and discovering the missing coin? They could be. Do you?"

I nodded. "I do, yes. Think about it. Sherlock and Watson zeroed in on the water the instant we arrived in town. Then, as soon as we were tasked with trying to recover the missing coin, we find it, in the paws of an otter, no less. It's just too coincidental for me. Of all the cases the dogs and I have worked, this one has to be one of the strangest."

Jillian moved away from the shirts and approached a glass display case filled with various rings, pendants, and earrings. She was silent as she studied the contents.

"Let's assume you're right," my girlfriend suddenly said, as she straightened and turned to look at me. "Let's assume that he was looking for sunken ..." Jillian trailed off as she looked around the busy store. Not wanting to be overheard, she dropped her voice and continued. "Let's assume Mr. Carlton was looking for sunken treasure. How is that even possible? We're on the western coast of the United States. Did Spanish galleons even make it this far west?"

I automatically nodded. I even knew the answer to this question, and it was thanks to the research I had done five books ago for my alter ego, Chastity Wadsworth. I forget which book that was, but I do remember setting it back in the 18th century. I was just as surprised then as Jillian was now, to learn that after Spain finally colonized California, all Spanish ships traveling along the coast, and that included the Manila galleons, had to stop in Monterey. During the 250 years of trading that Spain did, nearly 30 galleons had been lost. I wish I would have remembered that earlier.

"You're kidding," Jillian exclaimed, as she suddenly lost interest in the jewelry case. "The ships had to stop here, in Monterey? Why?"

I shrugged. "I never really understood why. But, do you realize what this means?"

Jillian nodded. "There could be gold out there."

"We just learned that there could be sunken treasure out there," I reminded my girlfriend. "Try to look a little bit excited, okay?"

Jillian laughed, just as Harry and Julie wandered by.

"Did we miss something?"

"There's a better-than-average chance that Jack Carlton was looking for sunken treasure," Jillian quietly explained. "Zachary says that a number of Spanish ships stopped here, at Monterey, through the years. A number of them went down, so there could be a sunken ship out there."

Julie nodded. "In that case, it makes perfect sense that only a highly skilled diver would try and search for such a ship. That must be incredibly dangerous."

Harry snorted. "I'll say. Jules, it killed the guy."

"No, it didn't," I corrected. "That neurotoxin probably killed the guy."

"He died by drowning," Harry argued.

"A professional master diver drowned? While wearing a tank of air on his back? Seriously, Harry?"

"Hey, it could happen."

"It could, but it didn't," I insisted. "That tetrodotoxin would have caused paralysis. If you can't move, then you can't swim. That's probably what got him."

I turned to reach for a baseball cap, with the words Monterey Bay across the front, when I thumped into someone I hadn't known was there.

"Whoops, my bad," I immediately apologized. "I didn't see you ..."

"Mr. Anderson!" a friendly voice announced, as I trailed off. "What a surprise!"

It was Chet Mayberry, coin collector extraordinaire.

"Hey there, Chet. How are you?"

Another guy appeared next to Chet, holding a light green shirt with a manta ray on it. He was about the same age, in his early fifties, lean as a rail, had chestnut brown hair, and a neatly trimmed beard. He noticed me staring and looked back at Chet.

"Do you know this man?" he politely asked, in a guarded voice.

"Of course. This is Zack Anderson. His wonderful dogs located my missing coin."

The calm, guarded demeanor was quickly replaced by a smiling, friendly face.

"How nice! I was just telling Chet how much I'd like to meet you. Oh, I don't see your dogs. Are they here with you?"

I looked back at Chet and waited for him to make the introductions. When nothing was forthcoming, I held out my hand to the newcomer.

"I'm Zachary Anderson. And you are?"

The newcomer sighed, shook his head, and grasped my hand.

"You'll have to forgive my husband. Chet's mind is probably already off somewhere else, thinking about coins. I'm Roger Parrish. I'm delighted to meet you. You made my Chet's day with the return of that blasted coin."

Jillian appeared by my side.

"Roger, this is Jillian, my girlfriend. Jillian? This is Roger, Chet's husband."

"How do you do?" Jillian politely asked. "What a surprise, bumping into Chet here, of all places. I would think the locals would avoid us tourists."

Roger grinned at us and shook his head. "To be honest, we usually do. However, Chet ruined one of my shirts when he used it as a polishing rag," he said, as he gave a stern look at Chet, who smiled and shrugged sheepishly. "This store, while trendy, and way too crowded for my tastes, does offer some fantastic prices." Roger held up three shirts. "Since the one he ruined is no longer here, Chet gets to buy me three new ones. In fact, I have a great idea. Since you returned his missing coin to him, and I've had to listen to him prattle on and on about how glad he is that it has been returned, he's going to buy you your hat and shirt as well."

I looked down at the two items I had been holding and fought the urge to whip them behind my back.

"Hey, I appreciate the thought, but that really isn't necessary. I was going to ..."

Like magic, the items I was holding vanished from my hands and reappeared in Roger's.

"I insist. It's the least you could do, isn't it, Chet? I mean, did you even offer these poor people a reward for returning your coin?"

Chet's eyes widened, as though he was a deer and had just been caught in a pair of headlights.

"I, er, no. I didn't. Well, I should ..."

I held my hands up in a time-out gesture.

"Just a minute, guys. While I appreciate the gesture, a reward isn't necessary. We're here on vacation, and thus far, it's been a memorable one. You really don't need to give us anything. In fact, I was going to ask you two if you drink wine."

Roger nodded. "Of course. Who doesn't?"

Jillian hooked a thumb at me. "Him."

It was Roger's turn to look surprised. "Oh."

I waved off his concern.

"The reason I ask is that, in Oregon, I own my own winery. Do you like Syrah? That's what my winery is known for. If you start giving me stuff, then I'll do the same for you two."

"Now I'm intrigued," Roger admitted. "I can say

I've had my share of wine over the years."

"Cases and cases," Chet confirmed, chuckling. "He is to wine, as I am to my coins."

"I still know more about coins than you do about wine," Roger good-naturedly accused.

"True."

"What winery?" Roger finally asked.

"It's called Lentari Cellars," Jillian answered for me. "We're from Pomme Valley, Oregon. It's a small little town in the southwestern section of the state.

"Lentari Cellars," Roger repeated. "I don't think I know that one. But, never fear. I do now. I'll be sure to pick up a bottle when I see one."

I looked over at Chet and realized I had the perfect opportunity to ask him something that I had been wanting to know.

"Chet, you obviously know your own coin, right?"

Chet nodded.

"That coin I gave back to you. Was it in the exact same shape as when you reported it stolen?"

Chet was already shaking his head, as though he had anticipated the question.

"Heavens, no. Then again, it's to be expected. If what you say is true, and an otter was using it to break open shells, then you can imagine that damage can and will occur."

"What's different about it?" Roger suddenly asked, interested. "The level of details on the coin's face, is that it?"

Chet nodded, pleased, "Yes. If the coin encountered any currents in the ocean, and was dragged over the surface of any rocks..."

"...or if an otter used it to open his dinner," I added.

Chet grinned at me and nodded. "Exactly. Wear and tear is to be expected."

"I guess what I'm asking," I lamely continued, as I struggled to search for the proper way to phrase my question, "based on how long the coin hasn't been in your possession, could a period of eight months change the coin's appearance as much as it has?"

Chet slowly nodded. "I see where you're going with this. Yes, there are some major differences. The detail on the castles has been greatly diminished. The mint mark is no longer as crisp as it used to be. It took me quite a while to remove all the sediment that had built up on it."

"Can that much deposit build up in such a short amount of time?" Roger asked.

Chet shrugged. "It's hard to say. No one has really done an experiment on a coin that age to see how it would break down in seawater. But, based on personal experience, I will have to admit that I would have guessed that coin had been submerged in water for at least two hundred years."

"Is there any way I could get a picture of it?" I asked. "I'd love to be able to show people what I found and that it could be part of a pirate treasure."

"Pirate treasure?" Roger repeated. "Where in the world did you hear that?"

"It's based off all the research I've done for one of the books I've published. Monterey used to be a stopping point for many Spanish ships in the 18th century, after Spain colonized California."

Roger snapped his fingers. "Right. I had forgotten. Well, since you asked, I can send you a copy of what Chet sent me yesterday, when he announced his coin had been returned. He sent me a picture to confirm it."

"I couldn't help it," Chet grinned. "I was in a good mood."

Jillian smiled warmly at the coin collector and his husband as I pulled out my cell and handed it to Roger. A few moments later, a new text message had arrived, and voila! I had a picture of the coin I had—ahem—stolen from an otter.

As we bade our goodbyes and exited the gift shop, my cell rang. At least, I thought it was mine. Seeing nothing on my display, I looked at my girlfriend.

"For once, that's you."

"Oh. Let me see who it is ... it's Julie. Hi, Julie! We were just leaving the ... what? What's wrong? Slow down. What's going on?"

Concerned by the worried tone of voice Jillian was now using, I gently pulled us out of the steady stream of foot traffic and guided us to an empty bench nearby.

"No, I'm sure everything will be okay. All right.

Stay there. I'll be right over."

Jillian finished the call and looked at me with concern evident on her face.

"That was Julie. She and Harry had a huge fight, which resulted with Harry storming off. She sounds like a mess right now. I'm sorry, Zachary. I have to go to her."

"At what point did they wander off to have their fight?" I curiously asked. "I mean, they were just with us a few moments ago."

"I don't know, Zachary. Oh, I have a bad feeling about this."

I held out my hand. "Give me Watson. You go take care of Julie."

"What are you going to do?"

I held up my phone and tapped the display.

"I was thinking about returning to the library to see if I can learn anything else about this coin."

"Shouldn't you go after Harry?" Jillian asked.

I shook my head. "If Harry got mad enough to steam off in a huff, then we should let him calm down. There's someone who doesn't react well to bad news. The question I'm wanting to know is, what bad news was he given?"

"I'd like to know that, too," Jillian confessed. "I don't understand what happened. They were getting along so well."

"Go see what you can do," I suggested. "If you need me for anything, then just give me a call. Where are you going to be?"

"Julie is down at the water, near the location

where we first found the body."

"Even with my supremely terrible sense of direction, I'll be able to find you. If not, well ..." I held up my phone, "... I'll cheat."

Jillian gave me a brief hug before hurrying off.

The library, I knew, was a little bit longer of a walk, and granted, I probably should have used my ridesharing app, but it was nice outside, and I didn't mind the walk. Neither did the dogs. Besides, it gave me time to think. More specifically, about just what was going on with my good friend, Harry? Why weren't the two of them getting along? Was there something he wasn't telling me?

Back at the library, and armed with a photo of the coin I was researching, I quickly found a website that specialized in locating and cataloguing shipwrecks. All you had to do was enter some search parameters, like the year(s) you were interested in, the geographic location, and so on, and the website would produce a list of shipwrecks known to include those coins.

Inputting 'Spanish galleon' under keywords, '1721' for the year, and 'California' for location, I hit Search and sat back in my chair, eager to see what results would appear. As I mentioned before, there were several wrecks that happened along the Pacific Coast. There, directly in front of me, were two good possibilities, and as I read through the specifications of each of them, my excitement grew. I gave each of the dogs a thorough scratching behind the ears and settled down to read.

Both dogs slid into down positions and elected to watch the people milling about.

The two results that appeared on my screen were for different ships. The first was nicknamed Wax Galleon. It was so named because, for hundreds of years, huge chunks of wax kept washing ashore. These large slabs of wax were then carbon dated, and discovered to be from the late 1600s.

It was very unlikely that this was the ship I was looking for, due to the location involved, namely the Oregon coast. Why, then, would it appear amidst the results when I searched for California? Because chunks of beeswax had washed ashore as far south as Northern California. However, the general consensus was that, somewhere in Oregon, there was a shipwreck containing thousands of pounds of beeswax, and that it was about 500 miles north of where it should have been. So, this couldn't be our ship.

The second, more promising result was for a ship called *San Augustin*. In the year 1735, *San Augustin* departed Manila, en route for Acapulco, Mexico. Loaded with spices, silk, gems, and even some porcelain from the Ming Dynasty, this 200-ton ship was supposed to have been wrecked in a place called Drake's Bay, which would have placed the ship roughly 170 miles from here. However, the wreck of the ship has never been found, and that certainly wasn't for a lack of trying.

Now, I will admit that there still was no definitive proof that the ship Chet's coin came from was the *San Augustin*. However, it was a fine suspect. The next question I wanted answered was, if found, could anyone lay claim to the ship?

The answer to that, thanks to the Abandoned Shipwreck Act of 1987, is a resounding no. The US government would hold title over any ship found within its territorial borders. Additionally, striking another nail in the coffin of any hopeful treasure hunters, if the shipwreck falls within the boundaries of any marine sanctuaries, or National Parks, then it was all but certain that the government would never allow salvage operations, regardless of how much treasure was at stake.

If Jack Carlton had located *San Augustin*, then no wonder he never told anyone about it. To do so would be akin to finding a huge treasure chest full of riches and then handing it to the government, saying, 'Here you go! Don't spend it all in one place.' There was simply no way our deceased diver was trying to pull this off by himself. He had to have an accomplice, but the question was, who?

Armed with my newly acquired knowledge, I texted Jillian to see if she was still down at the water. She replied almost immediately, which made me think she had been waiting for my message. Hopefully that didn't mean things were going badly with Julie and Harry. The last thing I wanted to see was another of our friends going through a painful divorce. On the plus side, though, the other friend of ours who had visited divorce court this year, Hannah, had finally had her divorce finalized and, thankfully, her attorney prevented her deadbeat husband from getting a single penny out of her. Then again, Jillian and I both pitched in to cover the cost of the attorney, and both of us opted to get the best one we could afford.

I found the girls sitting on the sand down at the beach. Much to my shock, Harry was with them! Also compounding my confusion was the fact that everything looked so normal. Harry and Julie were laughing together, while Jillian was smiling. Sherlock and Watson hurried over to the water's edge and, suddenly, I had my hands full with trying to prevent two dogs from diving nose-first into the water. Both corgis, I should add, gave me the stink eye when they realized a dip in the cool, refreshing water wasn't on the itinerary.

Jillian beamed a smile at me as I strolled up and cautiously sat down on her left. After a few minutes, Sherlock trotted over and gave my hand a lick, while Watson climbed into my lap and promptly went to sleep. I guess I was forgiven? Or else it was a 'We apologize in advance for what is about to come' gesture. I sincerely hoped it was the former. Just then, a family strolled by, caught sight of the dogs, and stopped to ask if they could pet them. Five minutes later, after numerous belly rubs had been doled out, the dogs' admirers wandered off. Jillian stroked Watson's red and white fur for a few moments before giggling.

"I don't know if these two dogs have ever had so much exercise and attention," Julie said. "Practically everyone that walks by wants to stop and say hello to them."

"And you noticed we're ignored," I guessed.

"Completely, man," Harry agreed.

I looked over at my best friend from high school and studied his face. What, exactly, had happened? And why had he stormed off? And, more importantly, what had brought him back and had him acting like nothing had happened? Harry cracked a joke just then, which brought a peal of laughter from Julie. I immediately nudged Jillian's shoulder.

"Is everything all right? I wasn't expecting to find Harry here when I arrived."

"Everything is fine," Jillian assured me. "It was just a bad reaction on Harry's part."

"A bad reaction to what?" Harry asked, overhearing his name.

Jillian turned to Julie and held out a hand to me.

"Perhaps you'd like to fill Zack in on what happened? I know he was just as worried as I was, and now you two have confused the heck out of him."

Julie stretched out an arm and laid a hand over mine.

"I'm so sorry for getting you guys so worried. It was just bad timing, and a less than favorable reaction from Harrison, who has since apologized."

"I did, man. I didn't react well, and I'm truly

sorry."

"You didn't react well to what?" I wanted to know.

Harry grinned and handed me a cold beer, from who knows where.

"I'm gonna be a father again, bro!"

Of all the news I was expecting to hear, this was nowhere on the list. I broke out into a grin and quickly stood up, which caused everyone else to do the same. I held out a hand.

"Congrats, buddy. You had me worried there for a bit."

"Well, I was worried, too. We never planned on having more than two kids, but here we are, with number three in the oven."

"If you don't mind me asking," I began, "why did you react so badly to the news? Obviously you weren't expecting it, but most people don't freak out that way."

Harry cast a worried look over at Julie, who was all smiles.

"Go ahead, Einstein. Tell him. It's okay by me."

"If it's TMI," I said, as I raised my hands in the universal time-out gesture, "then feel free to say so and refrain from answering."

"It was nothin' like that, man. I, er, didn't do my math right and might've ..."

"*Might* have?" Julie repeated.

"All right. I kinda thought that maybe I wasn't the father."

"Oh, Harry, no!" I groaned. "You don't ever, ever

accuse a woman of cheating, especially your wife! Have I not taught you anything?"

A smug smile formed on Julie's face, "Didn't I tell you? Well, as soon as Harry realized he was the father, and he had flown off the handle for no good reason, then he apologized."

"You must be really good at apologizing," I mused. "Usually, when accusations like that are made, it'll take a token of appreciation before an apology is even considered. And I'm talking about an *expensive* token of appreciation."

"She already picked out a new set of earrings online," Harry confirmed. "Darn things were pricey."

"Dude, be glad she didn't pick two sets. She could have ... What are the dogs doing?"

We all stopped to look at the dogs, who were both at the end of their leashes and were staring at the water.

"The otters are back, aren't they?" I guessed.

"I don't see any," Jillian said, shaking her head.

"I don't, either," Julie added.

"They're not moving, they're not barking, and they're not even whining," I observed. "Something has attracted their attention. Whatever. Anyway, Jillian, I wanted to let you know that I think I might've identified the shipwreck we all suspect is out there."

Jillian clapped her hands delightedly. "Well done, Zachary! All right, which one is it?"

"I think it's the *San Augustin*. It sailed from the

Philippines in 1735, on its way to Mexico, but sank off the northern coast of the state. Now, all the sources seem to indicate that the galleon sank around 170 miles from here, but they never found the ship."

"The *San Augustin*," Harry repeated. "So, if someone finds a sunken ship, then that means they can keep whatever they find, right?"

I shook my head. "No. There are laws in place which state that any vessel found within the territorial boundaries of the United States will become property of the government."

"A treasure hunter does all the work of finding the wreck, and the government then swoops in and takes all the treasure?" Julie asked, frowning.

"That's why I think Jack Carlton was acting in secret," I added. "That's why it's so important to find the missing dive log. We need to find out who his partner was in this endeavor."

A loud, high-pitched bark got our attention. It was Sherlock, and he was standing at the water's edge, his short nub of a tail wagging like crazy. Curious, I leaned to the side to look around him. Ah, there they were. The otters were back.

"His friends have returned," Jillian announced.

I nodded. "I can see that. Let me guess. They want to play, and they're inviting the dogs."

"Actually, no," Jillian said. "I think we didn't see them before because they were all looking for food. I think it's lunchtime for them."

"I'd say it's lunchtime for us," Harry announced. "Who else is hungry?"

I shrugged. "I could go for some fish and chips. One would think it shouldn't be too hard to find a restaurant around here that has it on their menu."

As we all prepared to leave, I heard the steady whapwhapwhap start up, signaling the otters were preparing to enjoy their meal. I gave the leashes a gentle tug, to let the dogs know we were leaving, when I noticed neither dog had budged. I looked back at Sherlock and saw he was ignoring me and probably hadn't heard a word I said.

"Hey, don't ignore me," I told the feisty corgi. "That's rude. You, too, Watson. Come on, guys. We're leaving."

Once more, I was ignored.

"No, you can't take your otter friends home with us. They're having lunch. Now, shake a paw, okay? We need to ..."

I trailed off as I noticed the young otter from before. He was floating on his back, off to the side of the, er, raft ... group. I've just decided I hate calling a group of otters *raft*. Anyway, the young otter was off to the side of the rest of the group, floating on his back. On his belly was an assortment of culinary treats: clams, mussels, and one small crab. In his paws, I could see that the otter was holding a mussel. A rock was produced and after a few whacks, the shells were smashed, discarded, and the meat consumed.

I looked down at the dogs, who seemed eager to be released so they could frolic with their aquatic friends.

"Don't even think about it. They're all eating. You're not gonna mess that up."

I turned away and took about three steps before Sherlock's sharp bark had me looking back at him.

"Really? What was that for?"

A flash of light drew my eyes back to the rock the otter was holding. The first time I noticed the rock. Last time, there was only a tiny bit of metal reflecting light. This time around, it was the reverse. The vast majority of the rock's surface was metal. There were no doubts about what it was. Before I could bring this to the attention of the others, I noticed Jillian suddenly point at a different otter. Then Harry and Julie did the same. The four of us were all pointing in different directions. A close inspection of the group of otters revealed nearly half of them were using coins as their rocks.

A realization dawned. The *San Augustin*? It had already been found, just not by humans.

"Look!" Jillian exclaimed, as she noticed there were more otters with coins than with rocks. "There are coins everywhere! What's going on?"

"Isn't it obvious?" I chuckled. "Our missing galleon has already been found."

"By the otters," Julie breathed. "How in the world ...?"

"It's not unheard of," Harry argued. "Think about it, Jules. The otters are constantly foraging for food. That means they're always hunting and exploring, looking for anything they can eat. This group ..."

"... raft," I slyly corrected.

"Huh?"

"Raft. It's what you call a group of otters in the water."

"Thank you, Mr. PBS. This raft of otters has clearly encountered the wreck, and have discovered that those coins make great rocks."

"I'd love to know if those are the same coins," I quietly said. I eyed the dogs, but was rewarded with a smack on my arm from Jillian.

"Don't even think about letting Sherlock and Watson disturb those poor otters from their lunch."

"I wasn't. I was actually thinking about the best way to try and get those otters to give us those coins."

Harry, much to my relief, suddenly looked down at the dogs. I just knew that the same thought had occurred to my friend. And, mimicking Jillian, Julie punched her husband on the arm. She waggled a finger at him.

"Nuh-uh. Aggravating the local wildlife is out of the question. In fact, I'm pretty sure that it's a crime."

"So, what do we do?" Harry plaintively asked. "Those otters could be holding a fortune in rare coins! And look at them! Banging them away on those shells. We gotta stop 'em, man!"

Inspiration struck. I pulled out my cell and

looked up a number online. Satisfied, I punched in the number and waited for a human to answer the line. And, it took several minutes of navigating through an automated system before I finally encountered a live person.

"Thank you for calling Monterey Bay Aquarium. This is Sharon. How can I help you today?"

Adopting my friendliest tone, I plastered a grin on my face and tried to sound cheerful.

"Hi, Sharon. Listen, my girlfriend and I were there yesterday and met up with Mr. Jonathan Hawk. Is there any chance he's there today? I have a question to run by him."

"And whom should I say is calling?"

"Zachary Anderson, owner of Lentari Cellars, in Pomme Valley, Oregon. Tell him I have a favor for him, and if he's willing to help, I'll be willing to send him a few bottles of wine, his choice."

"Lentari Cellars? From Southwest Oregon? I've heard of your winery, Mr. Anderson. Tell you what. I'll put the call through right now, if..."

"If?" I suddenly burst out laughing. "Oh, I get it. You want a bottle, too, don't you?"

"I prefer Gewürztraminer, thank you."

"It's a deal, Sharon."

I took down her mailing address and promised to send a bottle as soon as I was back home.

"I'm putting you through now, Mr. Anderson. Have a wonderful day!"

I heard a few soft clicks as my call traveled through the aquarium's phone system.

"Jonathan Hawk speaking."

"Mr. Hawk, this is Zack Anderson. We met the other day. Do you remember me?"

"The police consultant. Of course I remember you. What can I do for you, Mr. Anderson?"

Hoo boy, how do I start?

"Umm, are you familiar with the wild otter population that lives in the area?"

"Somewhat. You want to talk about otters, Mr. Anderson?"

"Believe it or not, I do. I even think it might be related to Jack Carlton's death."

"I'm listening."

I mentally crossed my fingers and prayed the aquarium's director wasn't involved in Jack Carlton's death.

"Umm, how would you go about relieving a rock from an otter?"

"A rock? From an otter? Are you referring to the tool they use to open shellfish?"

"Yes, exactly."

"Why in the world would you want to do that?"

Here we go.

"Well, they, er, they may be using Spanish reales instead of rocks."

"Am I understanding you correctly? You believe a raft of otters might be using ancient Spanish coinage as a way of opening up a clam?"

There. He called the otters a raft and it didn't sound stupid. So why, then, do I have such a problem with it?

"Yeah, I know it sounds crazy, but yesterday, we recovered one coin from that same, er, raft, and it turned out to be a local numist's missing coin."

"Numist? Do you mean, numismatist?"

"Whatever word means coin collectors."

"Wait. You say that you found these otters to be in possession of a Spanish reale yesterday, and somehow you got it away from the otter?"

"It was actually a two reales coin," I recalled. "Dated from 1721. Does that help?"

"I'll be darned. And now, you claim the otters have more of these coins?"

"Yes," I confirmed. "And, I'd keep that to ourselves."

"How ... how in the world did the otters get those coins?"

"This is just a guess, Mr. Hawk, but I think ... I think the otters are the ones who found *San Augustin*."

EIGHT

Thirty minutes later, I was sitting inside the private office of Mr. Jonathan Hawk, Director of Monterey Bay Aquarium. He had risen up from behind his desk the moment I arrived, shaken my hand, and then promptly closed the door behind me. He pulled out a chair in front of his desk and took the leather executive's chair behind it.

"You mentioned to me on the phone that you had a picture of one of these coins?"

I pulled out my cell, opened my photos app, and then handed him my phone.

"All this time, we thought we had found a coin stolen from a local coin collector late last year. I realize, now, that we didn't. We simply found another coin that just happened to be minted in the same year. It's just a fluke, Mr. Hawk."

"Please. I told you before to call me Jon."

"Will do. So, Jon, what do we do? How do we get those coins away from the otters? Or do we? Even try, that is."

"Legally, my advice is to leave the otters

alone," Jon advised me. "Interacting with the local wildlife around here is strictly taboo. Monterey cops are just itching to make an example of any tourist foolish enough to try."

"Great," I groaned.

"I'm not finished. That's my official answer."

Comprehending, I nodded. "And your unofficial answer?"

Jon's voice dropped so low that I had to lean forward to hear him.

"Get those coins away from the otters, as quickly as you can."

I don't know what I was expecting to hear, but that wasn't it.

"Come again?"

"You heard me," Jon insisted. "Get those coins away from the otters."

"But … why the urgency?" I stammered. "Do you think they're going to eat them?"

"Think about it," Jon said, keeping his voice low. "If the general public learns that a raft of otters is using sunken treasure to break apart shellfish, what do you think will happen?"

I whistled as I suddenly pictured the pristine beach overrun with knuckleheads with metal detectors, amateur treasure hunters, and those who would prey upon anyone fortunate enough to locate a few coins. It would be chaos.

"I can see from your expression you just realized the same thing I did," Jon told me. "Here's what we're going to do. I'm going to have several of my staff put together a few buckets of seafood otters find irresistible. I'll send you instructions where to pick it up."

"Thanks, pal. I appreciate it."

"Just be careful," Jon warned. "Wild animals that are fed can become very aggressive. And don't expect the otters to take anything from you by hand. You'll be lucky if they come anywhere close to you. What you're looking to do is provide a steady source of food for the animals, so they end up feeling like they don't need their rocks, okay?"

"Got it. Hey, with regard to involving a few other staff members, I wouldn't tell too many people about this," I warned.

"Why? Wait. Do you think the presence of these coins is related to Jack Carlton's death?"

"What do you think? Every bit of research I've found thus far says that, typically, a Spanish galleon would hold 50-60 tons of these coins. What do you think the market value of that is?"

"I see what you mean. I'll make sure I ask several of my most trusted staff. You'd better get going, Mr. Anderson."

I held out a hand. "It's Zack. And thanks, Jon."

We shook hands and parted ways. Back outside, I briefly considered hailing a cab, as I walked down the front steps of the aquarium. Then again, by the time I looked up the number, placed the call, waited for it to arrive, and then took the short five-minute car ride, I could walk back to the hotel quicker. So, that's what I did.

Less than thirty minutes later, I pulled up in Jillian's SUV and prayed to whatever deities that existed that the contents of the two buckets I just picked up didn't spill. Rolling the windows down just before I climbed out, I retrieved the two buckets, carefully placed them on the ground, and then locked up. Jillian noted my arrival first.

"Zachary! That was quick. What ... is that the car? You pulled it out of valet parking? And what do you have there, in the buckets?"

I set the buckets down in front of the dogs, who took an immediate liking to them, and took Sherlock's leash from Jillian. I waved over Harry and Julie, who were wandering the beach, looking for more pieces of sea glass. Unfortunately, they didn't find any.

"What's up, bro? Did you find out what we should do? Holy crap, man. What's in the buckets? It stinks to high heaven."

"It's raw seafood," I explained, "and you should see what it smells like in an enclosed car."

Jillian's eyes narrowed. "Zachary, you didn't."

"I'm sorry, I had to. I'll get your car detailed, inside and out."

"Did you lower some windows, so it'll air out?"

I nodded. "I did. Here's your keys, by the way. Now, listen up, everyone. I told our friend Jon, at the aquarium, about our situation here. He agrees with me, in that he believes the otters have found the *San Augustin*."

"The otters found the shipwreck," Julie softly

said, as she clutched her husband's hand. "I wouldn't have called that one."

"You and me both," I agreed.

"What are we supposed to do now, man?" Harry asked. He sniffed loudly and looked disdainfully down at the two buckets. "You called the aquarium. What do they want us to do, feed them?"

"They strongly advised that we do absolutely nothing," I relayed. "But, the director of the aquarium does recognize the danger in allowing these otters to have these coins. If the public were to catch on that the otters were using authentic Spanish coins from the 18th century, what do you think would happen to this area?"

"It'd be overridden with treasure hunters," Jillian guessed.

"People would go bat-crap crazy," Harry added, at the same time.

I nodded. "Precisely. Therefore, I've been advised, off the record, to try and get those coins away from them. How? The old-fashioned way: bribery."

"What do you plan on doing?" Harry asked, bewildered. "Swim out there and say, hey, bud, here's a tasty clam. Want to trade?"

I shrugged. "You never know until you try."

"Now would be a good time to do just that," Jillian suggested. "For the most part, we seem to be alone."

Harry pointed at the dogs, "Didn't you say that

the dogs spooked them yesterday? And that the otter dropped the rock it had been holding? What do you say we ..."

"No," I interrupted. "The guy at the aquarium says that, while playful, otters can be very aggressive, especially after they're fed. We're going to leave the dogs out of it for now."

I took off my shoes and socks, popped off the lid to one of the buckets, and almost gagged. Wow. If you think room temperature fish smells bad, you should try throwing in some raw sea urchin, handfuls of mussels, geoduck clams, and a few other things I couldn't identify. Plus, Jon advised me to simply keep the food flowing, and hopefully that alone would inspire the otter to drop its rock. At no time did I expect I'd have to feed any of the fuzzy critters by hand.

Wrong. I was mugged.

Let me explain. As soon as I stepped up to the water and popped the lid off the first bucket, all activity in the water ceased, only I didn't notice that at the time. Reaching into the bucket to retrieve a handful of mussels, I was about ready to fling them into the water when my first customer arrived for dinner.

The otter was an adult male, with a thick, dark brown undercoat and jet black guard hairs. It clumsily pulled itself out of the water, looked at the bucket and then back at me. A moment later, it had reached the bucket and, had I not been gripping the handle tightly, would have tipped it over. Using the bucket to steady himself, the otter pulled himself up onto his hind legs, looked over the rim at the contents below, chirped twice, and began making his selections, as though we were at the Golden Corral.

Once the first fellow hurried off, the second approached. And then the third. Before I knew it, I was surrounded by the raft of otters, only now, since they were on land, it meant they had become a romp. Whatever. I just knew I had to be careful. Some of the adult otters were easily three times the size of the corgis. I had no idea otters could get so big.

"Zachary!" Jillian suddenly called. "Look by your left foot!"

I risked a quick look down. Well, would you look at that! One of the otters had obligingly dropped its rock by my feet. Now we're talking. If only the others would follow suit, then I'd say ...

"Uh-oh," I heard Julie say.

"What's the problem?" I asked, while maintaining eye contact with the otters.

"Three of the otters on your left are no longer holding their rocks."

"What if they put them back in that storage pouch thing they have under their arms?" I asked.

Julie nodded. "I guess it's possible ..."

"... which doesn't help us," I grumbled.

"... or you could believe me when I say I watched them drop them into the water."

Well, I'll be a monkey's uncle. This was working?

"What about the rest of them?" I gently inquired, as the otter buffet line continued to attract customers. "I didn't think this would go over that well. I ... uh, oh. Harry? Give me the other bucket. Quick!"

The current customer, who just so happened to be Sherlock's friend, the youngster who dropped the original coin to begin with, looked imploringly at the empty bucket and then up at me. After a few moments, the otter pup cooed a few times and was about ready to bolt back to the water when Harry arrived. The otter watched me remove the lid and toss it aside.

"Come on, pal. I've got all kinds of stuff in here for you."

The pup watched me closely for a few seconds before I swear it shrugged and reached for the bucket. Selecting an urchin that had been split open, one small squid, and several clams, the pup retreated to the safety of the water, where it maneuvered itself so that it was floating on its back and using its belly as a table.

"He selected clams," Jillian observed. "Won't he need his rock for that?"

"They're already split open," I told her. "Those guys at the aquarium think of everything. Can you tell if he dropped his rock?"

"I'm sorry," Jillian apologized. "I should have been watching him, only I wasn't."

"I was," Julie said, stepping in. "Yes, he dropped

his rock, too."

"Are there any left holding coins?" I quietly asked.

My three friends shaded their eyes and studied the otters.

"I don't see any," Jillian reported.

"I don't, either," Julie added.

"I think they're all gone, man," Harry said.

"Now, we just need someone to go in the water and retrieve them," Julie said.

"I'll do it," Harry said, raising a hand. "Zack went in last time. It's my turn."

Harry stripped off his shirt and slid his shorts down. Sure enough, he was wearing swimming trunks underneath his clothes. Had he been planning on going into the water today? Seeing my confused expression, Harry shrugged.

"Hey, you never know if you're gonna have to go in the drink. What with the dogs, I just wanted to be sure."

Surprised, I looked at Jillian, whose emotions mirrored mine. Grateful beyond belief that I wasn't the one who would be getting wet, I suddenly remembered something that might come in handy. I held out a hand to Jillian.

"Would you mind passing me the car keys?"

Jillian fished them out of her purse, "Of course. What do you need them for?"

I handed the keys to Julie.

"If you look in the back of the car, you'll find a couple of towels. I always take them along whenever I travel with the dogs. Just in case. And before you ask, yes, they're clean."

"You're a lifesaver, Zack. I'll be right back."

"That was nice of you," Jillian observed.

Harry surfaced and tossed two of the otters' rocks to me. Taking a deep breath, my friend's head disappeared beneath the surface. I hooked a thumb in his direction.

"No, he's doing me a solid favor. I'm not sure what brought it on, but since I knew he'd be needing a towel, I figured he could use one of the dogs'."

Fifteen minutes later, Harry stood next to us, hurriedly toweling off as fast as he could go. His teeth were chattering and he was wheezing from his exertions.

"I d-don't know if th-those are all of 'em, m-man," Harry said, through clenched teeth. "I d-don't know h-how you d-did it earlier, b-buddy. Th-that water is as c-cold as a w-witch's t-t ..."

Julie suddenly held a finger to Harry's mouth, silencing him on the spot. She gave her husband a warm smile and waggled a finger at him. Right about then, we noticed the otters had disappeared. It was understandable. With Harry in the water, I'm sure they didn't want to stick around. Plus, they had full bellies. They were probably looking for a suitable place to go to sleep.

"What are we going to do with that?" Jillian asked, as she pointed down at the second bucket. "It's still half full. Should we give it back?"

Shrugging, I pulled out my cell and was put almost immediately through to Jonathan Hawk.

"Mr. Anderson. Dare I ask how it went?"

"Mr. Hawk. You had a heckuva suggestion. It went off without a hitch."

There was a brief moment of silence. I could only imagine my new friend, Jon, was now sitting up straight in his chair and had given me his full attention.

"The coins? The rocks? You've got them?"

"We have nine of them," I confirmed. "Plus, we have a half full bucket of leftover food. The otters are all gone, and I was wondering what you'd like me to do with it."

"Dump it. It cannot come back to the aquarium. In layman's terms, the contents have been compromised by wild otters. I can't risk exposing any of my animals to anything they might be carrying."

"I understand. Harry? Would you dump this out over there? Just dump it in the water. It'll be gone before you know it."

"Mr. Anderson? Er, Zack? Could I ask a favor?"

"You've already done me a solid favor today. If I can, I'll do the same for you."

"Would you bring a few of the coins to me here? A couple of us, myself included, are dying to take a look at them."

"Sure. We'll rinse this bucket out and then head over. Oh, wait. I have to stop by the hotel first. I have my dogs with me."

"Oh? What kind of dogs are they? I ask only because I'm a dog lover. I always have been."

"Corgis."

"Corgis? Pembrokes or Cardigans?"

"You know your dog breeds. They're Pembrokes. They're the ones without a tail."

"One moment, please. Shannon, are you out there? Would you come here for a second?"

"Is everything okay?"

"We have an intern here who absolutely loves corgis. She has them on her keychain, on her car, and has pictures of them on her purse. To say she is a fan of the breed is an understatement. If you want to just come here, then I know she would be thrilled to watch them for you."

"Oh, I get it. Perfect. We'll be over shortly."

"I'll be waiting."

Twenty minutes later, we were in a staff-only parking lot behind the aquarium. Being the last of the four to follow the director inside, I turned behind me to watch the short, blonde woman playing with my dogs. From what I had been told, the girl had practically cried when asked if she'd puppysit two corgis for a little while. In the last five minutes, I watched the girl take at least a dozen selfies with the dogs.

Once we were inside the director's office, we were introduced to the head curator, a redheaded, bearded fellow by the name of Randall Foster. Also present was a middle-aged brunette by the name of Meredith Barnes, whom we were told was the head of animal husbandry, whatever that meant.

Jon spread out a large yellow towel across his desk and indicated it was where I should put the specimens we collected. Placing four of the otter 'rocks' on the desk, I stepped back and allowed the aquarium officials to begin their study. Almost immediately, the excitement level increased as each of the four samples were examined.

"This one is a Spanish reale," Randall commented. "I can't quite make out the date, other than it's 17- something. Maybe 1725? We'd have to remove all this sediment here if we wanted to know for sure."

"This one has a date of 1719," Meredith reported. "But, that's about the only thing I can make out. The markings are similar, so I have to assume this is also a Spanish reale."

"The coin we first recovered was a two-reale coin," I added. "I'm not sure how many denominations they come in."

"Neither am I," Jon admitted. "I'm sorry to say I slept through most of my archaeology classes. I found it utterly boring."

Randall grinned at his boss and pointed at the four coins.

"And now? Do you still find it boring?"

"Not when it's dropped in my lap like this."

"Any chance Jack Carlton might have been working to discover the location of the *San Augustin*?" I asked. "I'd say it's too tempting to pass up. If what we've heard is true, and he was always diving out there, then logic would suggest ..."

"Who told you that?" Randall inquired, looking up at me. "Jack didn't like diving in Monterey. Plus, he really didn't have time for it. We saw him maybe three months out of the year at most."

Meredith nodded. "Agreed. If Jack had known these coins were being used as rocks by the otters, then he would more than likely have brought NGC here and filmed a special about it."

"NGC?" Harry repeated uncertainly. "What's that, man?"

"You've probably heard of it," Meredith answered, giving Harry a smile. "It's an acronym, short for National Geographic Channel. Jack was one of their top divers."

"She's right," Jon announced. "Jack would've turned the discovery of a shipwrecked treasure ship into a media frenzy. This all but confirms he had nothing to do with this."

I mentally snapped my fingers. So much for that theory. If Jack wasn't involved, then what was he doing out in that water?

"Don't forget, he was found in that same area," I reminded everyone. "If he didn't know about it, then what was he doing out there? And, more importantly, who was he diving with?"

"He's got a point," Randall admitted. He placed the coin he had been studying back on the desk. "Jon, I'd say this definitely confirms it. *San Augustin* has been located, but just not by any of us." Randall caught me staring at him and he shrugged.

"I minored in archaeology."

Jillian raised her hand. "I have a question."

Jon looked her way and nodded. "Yes, Ms. Cooper. Go ahead."

"Do you have any animals here that contain tetrodotoxin?"

The room fell silent.

"Why do you ask that?" Jon quietly asked.

Surprised, Jillian looked at me.

"We had assumed you guys were told," I gently told the three members of the aquarium's staff.

"We were told what?" Jon asked. "Are you saying tetrodotoxin was found in Jack's bloodstream?"

"About four milligrams of it," I recalled. "That's what the police told me."

Alarmed, Jon looked over at Randall and his face became grim.

"Go. Check on them. I want a complete tally of all of them."

Randall nodded. "I'm on it." He then hurried out of the room.

"What's going on?" Meredith asked, confused. "What's he going to check?"

"He's checking on the one species in this facility," Jon slowly explained, "that just so happens to be labeled as one of the most venomous creatures living in the water: the blue-ringed octopus. Its sting is lethal and contains tetrodotoxin."

Jillian gave a soft gasp and she clutched my arm.

"I ... I thought this facility only focused on marine life living in the area?" my girlfriend tremulously asked.

"We do focus on local sea life," Jon admitted, "but we also have species from other parts of the world."

"Are there any other species here that contain this neurotoxin?" I asked.

Jon shook his head. "No. Just the one."

"How many of them do you have?" Julie asked. "I'm surprised you'd want to put something like that on display if it's so dangerous."

Jon shrugged. "It's no different than a regular zoo maintaining a rattlesnake exhibit."

Julie nodded. "That's true. I hadn't thought about that."

"And, like a zoo," Jon continued, "whenever there's a dangerous species involved, only highly qualified keepers are allowed to handle the animals."

"Was Jack one of those people?" I asked.

Harry grinned. "Oooo, good question, Zack."

Jon looked over at Meredith.

"You personally selected and trained the staff who'd be handling those toxic animals. Was Jack Carlton one of them?"

Meredith sadly nodded. "He was. But, I should also like to point out that his responsibilities lay elsewhere, and not with those octopuses. He may have been cleared to open that exhibit, but I'm fairly certain he never did."

"I want a list of names of all ..."

"Excuse me, Mr. Hawk," Meredith interrupted. "Let's not jump to conclusions. Not yet, anyway. Let's give Randall enough time to check the exhibit."

"Check the exhibit for what?" I wanted to know. "How many of those things do you have?"

"We started with one female and one male," Jon said.

"Started with?" Jillian repeated. "And now?"

"They had babies," Jon reported. "We were the first aquarium to begin a captive breeding program for the blue-ringed octopus. Several months ago, their first clutch hatched, but only a handful survived."

Not being particularly fond of quiet rooms, I felt compelled to keep the conversation going. However, the only thing I could think to talk about was the situation at hand.

"Umm, how dangerous are these octopuses?" I hesitantly asked. "I mean, I heard you say they were venomous, but are they as deadly as, say, a black widow spider?"

"More so," Jon immediately answered.

I'm sure my eyes bugged out a little and I know I paled, because I felt the blood drain out of my face.

"Can one of these things kill a man?" Jillian asked.

Jon nodded. "Yes. Depending upon the amount of neurotoxin that enters the bloodstream, death can happen within minutes."

"But that diver," Harry protested, "the autopsy report ... it said that the cause of death was drowning. Sea water was found in his lungs."

"A sting from an adult will more than likely kill you," Jon patiently explained. "But, if for some reason, the amount of neurotoxin wasn't that severe, then, I'm sorry to say, paralysis would occur."

"That's why he drowned," I said, as I shuddered. "He was stung by one of those things and became paralyzed, obviously underwater. What a horrible way to go."

A two-way radio I hadn't noticed before suddenly squawked to life on Jon's desk.

"Jon H, this is Randall. Come in please."

Jon snatched up the radio.

"I'm here."

"Would you please report to MBH? Thank you."

I looked at Jon. "MBH?"

"Monterey Bay Habitats. It's where we keep individual tanks, and consequently, the blue-ringed octopuses."

"We should probably get out of your hair," I suggested, drawing affirmative nods from the rest of my companions.

Surprisingly, Jon shook his head. "You're more than welcome to join us. If I find what I think I'm going to find there, then you've helped to uncover a breach in our security, and that is something I won't tolerate."

We followed Jon and Meredith on a direct course for the section of the aquarium titled Monterey Bay Habitats. Ducking into a short hallway, Jon pulled out his key ring and unlocked the Staff Only door. Ushering us inside, he quickly closed the door to several members of the public, who had been curiously watching us.

After taking a few sharp turns, which led to several narrow passageways between a variety of bubbling tanks of seawater, we arrived at a familiar spot. There, just ahead of us, was the doorway to the three offices we had visited earlier, with the deceased Jack Carlton's office on the left and two others on the right. Randall was there, along with another staff member. This one was a woman, about the same age as me, and was short, had shoulder-length black hair, and wearing a very discernible frown on her face.

Jon strode straight over to Randall.

"What's the count? You've called me here, so I can only assume something's off."

"Both adults are accounted for," Randall reported.

"And the babies?" Jon asked, as the tone of his voice grew angry.

"I counted fourteen."

"Oh, dear God," Jon breathed. "That cannot be. Check again."

"I did," Randall insisted. "I counted them all, three times. Then I brought Kathy in and had her count. She came up with the same number I did, each time."

Jon looked over at the woman, Kathy, and then realized introductions needed to be made.

"I'm sorry. This is Kathy Sutherland. She's head of MBH. Nothing happens down here without her knowledge."

"Nothing ever has," Kathy quietly stated. "Until today."

"What's going on?" I asked. "You're missing one of those babies, aren't you? Would a sting from a young octopus be enough to kill?"

"It didn't have to be enough to kill," Jillian reminded me. "It just had to be enough to paralyze. The open water took care of the rest."

"Are we missing one of the juvenile, blue-ringed octopuses?" Meredith asked.

"There should be fifteen," Jon confirmed. "One of our blue-ringed octopus juveniles has gone missing!"

NINE

Can you believe this is happening?" Jillian whispered in my ear. "They've closed the entire aquarium! All on account of this missing octopus. This is spooky!"

"Did you hear what they said about that octopus?" I reminded her. "That thing is one of the deadliest creatures to live in the sea. There's enough tetrodotoxin in one of those tiny octopuses to kill 26 adults within minutes. That's not something you want to screw around with, let alone admit someone made off with one."

"I couldn't agree more," Jon solemnly said, as he appeared by my side. "I simply cannot believe that one of our staff took a juvenile octopus. The ramifications of this are ... staggering. I can't even begin to fathom the amount of bad press this is going to generate."

"I know you guys have security cameras outside," I began, "but I'm guessing there aren't any behind the scenes here?"

Jon shook his head. "No. I've petitioned for a security system for years now, but the public never wants to fund things like that. The only thing they like seeing is the addition of more exotic animals. That's why we have those blasted octopuses. The more dangerous an animal is, the more of a draw it is to the people. I just don't know what we're going to do."

"Let's start with this," I began. I looked over at Jillian and winked. Correctly guessing what I was about to do, she nodded, signaling her approval. "Contact some security companies. Get some estimates for a professionally installed security system, complete with cameras, off-site data backup, remote access, and so on."

"That would cost a fortune," Jon lamented. "We won't be able to put anything else to a vote until early next year."

I shook my head. "No, you don't understand. Get some estimates. Jillian and I will cover the bill. Consider it a private donation."

"While I appreciate the thought," Jon began, "you have no idea how much a proper security system can run. I wouldn't want to impose on ..."

"We insist, Mr. Hawk," Jillian added. "It's our gift to the aquarium. That way, if you're pressured to respond to public outcry, then you can tell them that, to avoid incidents like this in the future, a top-of-the-line security system is being installed. It'll make the people feel better."

"You do realize that a system like the one you're describing will probably cost upwards of a million or two?"

We both nodded. Jon's eyes bugged out.

"Seriously? You're okay with that?"

"We are."

"Wow. Thank you both."

"We're not as loaded as these two, but we'd like to help, too," Harry added, drawing a nod of approval from Julie.

"Then it'll be from the four of us," I announced.

"That ... that's a relief," Jon finally admitted. "I wasn't too sure how to handle the press, but I think you've got us on the right track. Now, if we could only locate Jack's dive log, we might be finally able to put everything to rest."

"It's probably long gone by now," Julie decided.

Jon confidently shook his head.

"Believe it or not, we think that book is still in here. Somewhere. We just don't know where."

"How can you be so certain?" Jillian asked. "Wouldn't whomever stole it want to move it as far away as possible from here?"

Jon nodded. "If they could get it away from this facility, then I'm sure that's exactly what they want to do. However, I have a feeling they haven't."

Seeing the confused looks on our faces, Jon patted the air.

"Let me explain. On the exact day we learned about Jack Carlton's death and discovered his office had been ransacked, we knew something was — and you must pardon the pun here — fishy. We instigated searches of all employees and volunteers who were leaving the facility. Backpacks, purses, and bags. Everything was checked. Did the dive log turn up? No."

"You think it was stashed somewhere in here," I guessed. I looked around at the myriad of places a small book could be hidden and groaned. "What are the chances you'll find it?"

"Slim to none," Jon admitted.

"Too bad you don't let dogs in here," Harry quipped. "Zack's two dogs could find your missing dive log in no time flat, man."

"How's that?" Jon curiously asked. "You're talking about the two corgis that Shannon is presently looking after? Are they trained police dogs?"

I shook my head. "No, I'm afraid not."

"I didn't think so," Jon said. "So, I'm afraid it'll be ..."

"You didn't let me finish," I interrupted. "They're not police dogs, no, but they are official consultants. I kid you not. They've solved quite a few cases up in Pomme Valley."

"Cases," Jon skeptically repeated. "Do tell."

"Sherlock kept his butt out of jail when Zack was arrested for murder," Harry helpfully supplied.

I watched Jon's eyes widen and I groaned.

"Couldn't you have started with a different case than that one?"

"You were arrested for murder?" Jon repeated, his eyes unblinking.

"I didn't do it," I confirmed. "I was set up. I had

just moved to town and found a dead person in my winery."

"Sherlock and Watson located a missing Egyptian pendant," Julie announced. "It was once owned by King Tut. It was very valuable and quite small, so it could have been hidden anywhere, yet Sherlock found it hidden in a tube of potato chips."

"Pringles," Harry clarified.

Jon grunted. "Hmm."

"Then Sherlock and Watson located a group of people responsible for stealing other people's dogs," Jillian said.

"Those two dogs solved Zack's late wife's murder," Harry added.

"They caught the people responsible for ..."

Jon held up his hands. "All right! Enough. I could ... I mean, I could simply say they were support dogs. Yeah, that'll work. Very well. Meredith? Would you go bring Shannon and the dogs here, please?"

Giving Jon a knowing smile, Meredith slipped away. A few minutes later, the young blonde, who had been dog-sitting my corgis, appeared. At her side were the PVPD's secret weapons, namely, my two dogs. The girl handed me the leashes, gave the dogs a thorough scratching behind the ears, and left.

"Okay, pal, you two are up. We're looking for a missing dive log. Now, I don't know if it's around here, or somewhere else in the aquarium, only..."

I trailed off as the leashes went taut. The dogs wanted to explore already. That was a good sign, wasn't it?

I gave the corgis as much leash as I could and carefully navigated around the narrow walkways and low-hanging pipes. Sherlock, content to take the lead, sniffed along the base of several tanks before snorting and moving on. Looking behind me, I could see that we had amassed quite a collection of followers. Besides the four of us, we had Jon, Meredith, Kathy, and three others I hadn't seen before, silently trailing behind.

Sherlock threaded his way through another series of tanks, pausing only to tilt his head at several gurgling pipes that were running along the floor. Then, he changed course and headed toward a closed door. I looked behind us, intent on asking Jon to unlock the door, when I realized the door must lead back outside, to the public viewing area. I tried the handle: it wasn't locked.

Walking through the eerily silent hallways, with the numerous tanks visible on either side of the walls, and with the distinctive briny seawater smell filling every nook and cranny, I followed Sherlock as he pulled me toward what had to be the other side of the wall from where we were standing. Sure enough, Sherlock paused to sniff along a bubbling twenty gallon tank. Looking inside, I could see two remarkably tiny octopuses, with dark rings on their bodies and tentacles. Weren't the venomous octopuses supposed to have rings on them? Did that make these two the proud parents of the missing juvenile?

Granted, I really didn't know what poisonous octopuses were supposed to look like, but what I saw in the tank didn't look particularly harmful to me. These were the dangerous critters carrying tetrodotoxin? These two octopuses were smaller than my hand and looked super photogenic. If I came across that in the wild, especially as a scuba diver, I'd be tempted to reach out and pet it. But, I also remember a little bit of my high school biology class, where my teacher informed us that the more vibrant the colors an animal had, the higher the risk of it being dangerous. Plus, I didn't see any baby octopuses anywhere. Perhaps they were being held in another tank?

Sherlock moved on. This time, he led me to a larger viewing area, where nearly a third of the room had a shallow, open water tank in it. Glancing in, I saw what looked like a manta ray, resting on the sandy bottom of the tank.

"It's a skate," Meredith explained, correctly guessing that I must have been wondering what type of animal it was. "It's perfectly harmless."

Nodding, I gathered up the leashes, intent on guiding the dogs away from the tank when I noticed both Sherlock and Watson had sat down. Sherlock looked at me, gave me a head tilt, and then stared back at the tank. Much to my surprise, the little tri-colored corgi reared up on his legs, so that he could get his nose up and over the rim of the tank. Watson followed suit a few moments later.

"Why are we here?" I heard Jon ask. "What are they doing? Zack, they really shouldn't be getting too close to the animals."

"You heard him," I scolded the dogs, giving the leashes a firm tug. "Come on, we're looking for something to do with ..."

I trailed off as I stared at the dogs, who were staring inside the tank. I wordlessly turned to Jillian, who shrugged, and then to Jon, I pointed at the tank.

"Can you tell if there's anything different about this exhibit?"

Jon stepped up to the tank, looked down at the quiescent skate, and then looked over at Meredith.

"Who maintains the skate exhibit?"

"I do," Kathy said, as she stepped around Meredith. "Is something the matter?"

Jon pointed at the tank, "You tell me. If you're the one who cleans this tank on a daily basis, then you'd be able to spot any differences, wouldn't you?"

Kathy shrugged, leaned over to study the tank, and immediately frowned.

"What is it?" Jon asked. "You frowned awfully quickly."

"She's spotted something," Jillian deduced.

Kathy nodded. "I have. That. That right there. Do you see that gray rock? It wasn't there two days ago when I vacuumed the sand."

I raised a hand. "Umm, could you run that by me again? Did you say you vacuumed the sand?"

"It's an underwater vacuum," Kathy explained. "There's not enough suction to suck up the sand, or small rocks, but bits of debris will be pulled in. Practically every aquarium utilizes some type of vacuum system to keep their underwater exhibits clean."

Jon pointed at the rock.

"Could that have been thrown in by a visitor?"

Kathy nodded. "Sure. I've seen that type of thing happen before. Want me to get it?"

"I would appreciate it," Jon said.

Kathy took off her boots, rolled up her pants, and waded into the water. The big skate, seemingly asleep up until this point, suddenly darted to the opposite side of the tank. Slowly reaching into the water, Kathy retrieved the rock and had taken a few steps back toward the edge of the large tank when she hesitated. She had rotated the rock in her hand and was now looking at the reverse side.

"Huh. Will you get a load of that?"

She held up the stone for us. Bits of metal flashed at us in the bright viewing area lights. The aquarist was holding one of the otter rocks!

Jon held out a hand. "Would you?"

Kathy passed it over, then stepped out of the tanks and started rolling her pants back down. "What is it? Why would there be metal on it?"

"Because this appears to be a 1720 Spanish two reales coin," Jon answered, unable to hide the astonishment in his voice. "I'll be darned." The director of the aquarium looked over at me, and then down at the dogs. "All right, you have me convinced. Sherlock, is it? Do you think you and your friend can find the missing dive log? If you can do that, then ... then ... I'll tell you what. Zack, if your dogs find that missing dive log, then I'll give you and your wife lifelong memberships to the aquarium."

"You're on," I said.

"I'm your wife now, huh?" Jillian whispered in my ear as she passed by me, holding Watson's leash.

My face flamed up. Had Jon called Jillian my wife? And I hadn't said anything to contradict him? Hoo, boy. What does that say about me? That'll have to be a conversation I save for a later day.

Feeling Sherlock tug at his leash, I increased my pace and allowed him to begin exploring once more.

"Someone knows," Jon's voice suddenly said, almost in my ear. I turned to see the aquarium director walking alongside me. "Someone here at the aquarium knows about *San Augustin*. I'd even go so far as to say they've probably located it. As for the skate exhibit? Someone placed that rock in there, in broad daylight."

"It was the perfect hiding place," I surmised.

"It's out in the open, and unless you knew what to look for, perfectly invisible in the big manta ray tank."

"Skate," Jon corrected.

"Whatever," I grinned. "Hey, where does that door lead?" I asked, as I pointed at a sturdy metal door with the top half made up of iron bars, allowing someone to see into the room. In this case, however, the room was dark.

"That? That's the equipment room. It's where we store scuba gear. Tanks, regulators, buoyancy control vests, weight belts, suits, and so on. Why do you ask?"

I silently pointed at Sherlock. He had stopped in front of the door and was staring at it, as though he had heard a strange noise coming from the other side. Without argument, the keys were produced and the door was unlocked. Stepping inside, we saw exactly what Jon had described: scuba gear, and it was everywhere. There were at least ten tanks lined up against the opposite wall. A metal shelving unit contained regulators and vests. Another shelving unit held several complete weight belts and quite an assortment of various weights. Diving knives, masks, fins, and just about anything else a diver would need was on the third wall. Sherlock, however, ignored all of it. He looked back at Watson, shook his collar, and turned to the left.

The far left corner of the equipment room held a large open crate. Inside were bright orange life jackets, the kind which you'd typically find stowed under the seat on a boat. The corgis trotted over to the crate, sniffed around the edges for a few moments, then promptly sat. I studied Sherlock, wondering yet again how he knew where to look. Was there something in the box besides life vests?

Jon was already at the crate. He was pulling out vests and handing them to Meredith, who stacked them in a neat pile nearby. Nearly a dozen life jackets later, Jon hit the bottom. However, there was nothing else to find. Jon gave me a quizzical look, but noticed I was still watching Sherlock. The corgi was now staring at the pile of stacked life vests.

What happened next had the entire room laughing. Jon proceeded to pick up a life vest, held it out to Sherlock, and when the corgi ignored it, tossed it back into the crate. Eight jackets later, Sherlock perked up as a life jacket that was seemingly identical to the previous ones was presented. Curious why that particular jacket had attracted Sherlock's attention, Jon gently squeezed each section of the jacket, pausing only when he hit the larger chest sections.

What was that song from *Sesame Street*? One of these things is not like the other?

Jon felt along the seams and carefully pried the Velcro apart. The jacket should have contained something along the lines of polyethylene foam, but that particular section contained something entirely different: a small padded green notebook. It was a match to the other four that had been in Jack Carlton's office, which meant ... it was the missing dive log!

"Hot dang!" I exclaimed. "Is that what I think it is?"

"It's a dive log," Jon confirmed. He flipped open the page and began to read. After a few moments, he was nodding. "It belongs to Jack, all right." The aquarium director knelt down next to Sherlock and gave him several scratches behind the ears. "Well done, boy. Good job!"

Sherlock's tongue flopped out and he panted contentedly. Watson whined once, as if to remind everyone that she helped, too. Jon patted her head and then looked over at me.

"You have some amazing dogs, Mr. Anderson."

"Oh, trust me, I know it. They know it. All of Pomme Valley knows it."

"They really do," Jillian confirmed, giving me a smile.

I pointed at the dive log. "Well? Don't keep us waiting. What's the last entry? Does it say where he was diving?"

Jon started flipping the pages, taking at least a dozen pages at a time as he rapidly searched for the last entry. Stopping at a page that was almost at the end of the book, Jon grunted once and began to read to himself. After a few moments, his eyebrows lifted and he grunted again. Finished reading, he closed the book and looked at the group of people looking eagerly back at him.

"It only says he was planning on going out into McAbee Bay," the director glumly said. After a few moments, a grin appeared. "But, it also says that he was diving in an undisclosed location, since one of his volunteers had insisted there was 'something worth his while' out there."

"One of his volunteers said that?" Meredith exclaimed. "Well, which one? Does it say?"

Jon shook his head. "No, unfortunately. But, it won't be that difficult to figure out."

"Why do you say that?" I asked.

"Because, Jack says, and I quote, 'she keeps insisting she found something that will impress me.' He doesn't say it, but I get the distinct impression that he did the dive only to humor her."

"How does this help us identify her?" I asked, confused.

"I can answer that," Kathy volunteered, raising a hand. "I know all the people who volunteer in this department. As such, I know Jack had at least six volunteers. Four of those volunteers are male. The other two are female."

"That surprises me," I admitted. "I thought for sure that, from the sounds of things, all his volunteers would be female."

"A while back, they were," Kathy admitted. "Then, one day, he called a meeting with me and Heather, who oversees all the volunteers. He said he wanted to eliminate all his existing volunteers and start over. I didn't know it at the time, but two of the volunteers were aggressively pursuing him, even though he was newly married. So, starting over, he carefully selected which volunteers would work in close proximity with him."

"That's why they're mostly male," Jillian guessed. "To remove the possibility of temptation?"

Kathy nodded. "Correct."

"If I do the math correctly," I slowly began, "then that means there are still two more volunteers, and they were both women. How would you explain that?"

Harry suddenly laughed out loud. "Hey, man. I can answer this one."

I nodded. "By all means."

"These two ladies? He figured they were harmless."

"He wasn't attracted to them at all," Julie translated. "Either that, or he felt there was no chance of anything ever happening."

"What are the names of the two female volunteers?" Jon asked, in a guarded voice.

"Well, there's Sherry VanZanten," Kathy began. "Nice girl, even though she's ... umm ... a bit quirky. And there's the other girl, a junior from the local high school. She's a minor, so I'll leave her name out of this for now. Sweet kid. She has to be one of the hardest workers I have ever seen. She hasn't graduated high school yet, but already knows what she wants to specialize in: cetacean biology."

"What kind of biology?" I asked, as I turned to Julie.

"Whales," Julie translated. "It sounds like she wants to work with whales."

Kathy nodded. "Correct. She's volunteered for every whale watching expedition we have ever undertaken, and she's made it expressly known that she wants to start her very own institute devoted to the preservation of whales."

"Which kinds?" I asked.

Kathy shrugged. "All kinds."

"That's impressive," Jillian observed. "To be that young and focused, at the same time."

"Which one do you think he was diving with?" I asked. "Are both of them certified divers?"

Jon looked over at Kathy, who nodded.

"Both are certified deep water divers."

I whistled, impressed.

"Deep water, huh? I never got that far in my own certification. I've only been down to about 35 feet or so."

"Deep water certification allows you to dive down to a depth of 100 feet," Jon explained. "All of Jack Carlton's volunteers were certified divers."

"So, it could be either of them," I guessed. Just then, I snapped my fingers. "Wait. Wait, wait, wait. Sherry VanZanten? Isn't that the name of the lady we found hiding in the bushes on the day of Jack's death? Holy crap! How could I have forgotten that! Of course it's her! Why else would she hide from us?"

Jon turned to Meredith and Kathy.

"Pull her contact information. We need to find out where she is. Plus, we'll need to inform the police."

"I still have Officer Adolphson's cell phone on my own cell," I helpfully supplied. "I can call her and give her an update."

"Thank you, Mr. Anderson. Oh, and Zack? Please go out and buy your dogs two of the most expensive treats you can find and send me the bill. I owe them my thanks."

Once the four of us ... oops. Did it again. Once the six of us were outside, I telephoned Mary and gave her an update. She didn't seem surprised. In fact, she told me that Sherry VanZanten was already a person of interest, and after being interviewed for nearly two hours straight, she promptly left the station and vanished. She wasn't answering her phone and she didn't report in for her regular job, which was as a paralegal.

I should have listened to my gut instinct. Sherlock had caught Ms. VanZanten hiding in the bushes after Jack's body had been discovered! I mean, how guilty could you get? And what had her excuse been? She was simply trying to compose herself and collect her thoughts? Because she had just learned about the death? I didn't buy it. And, clearly, neither did the local police.

Now that the police and Monterey Bay Aquarium had been alerted to the dangers of Ms. VanZanten, we decided our good deed for the day had been done and returned to the hotel. I wrapped the leashes tightly around my hand and angled for the hotel lobby, only the dogs had other plans. Sherlock immediately braked, bringing me to a swift, albeit unpleasant stop. Rubbing the kinks out of my already sore shoulder, I looked back at Sherlock and saw that both of them were sitting on the ground, staring straight at me, as if they couldn't believe what they were seeing.

"What? What's with you two? Knock it off. Come on, it's been a long day. We need to ..."

"Awwooooo!" Sherlock howled.

"What's the matter with him?" Jillian asked.

"I'm not sure," I said. I tried giving the dogs a friendly but firm tug on the leash, indicating I wanted to keep moving in the same direction we had been moving before we all stopped. However, as before, Sherlock refused to be swayed. Then, both dogs simultaneously rose to their feet and turned to look back at the nearby beach. Then I heard another whine. About ready to scold Watson, I suddenly realized that Sherlock was the one who had made that noise, not my timid, little female.

"Was Sherlock the one who just whined?" Harry asked, amazed. "I don't think I've ever heard him whine like that."

"That makes two of us," I agreed. "Sherlock? What's the matter? Let me guess. You want to play with your little friend down at the beach? That's probably not a good idea, pal. I've recently learned that those otters can be aggressive. Sure, they're playing with you now, but ... and you're both ignoring me."

Both corgis had turned to face the beach and were now sitting with their backs to me.

"Harry? Julie? Care to go for a walk? It sounds like there's something Sherlock wants us to see, so I'm going to take them outside for a bit. Jillian, would you care to join me?"

Jillian slipped her arm through mine, "Why, I thought you'd never ask. Want me to take Watson?"

I nodded. "Sure. Here."

With one dog each, we headed toward the water. However, before we could reach the water's edge, the dogs pulled us to a stop. Then, with their furry ears sticking straight up, reminding me of two miniature German Shepherds, Sherlock briefly turned to Watson before resuming his trek, only now we were angling north.

"Any idea where we're going?" Jillian quietly asked me.

"No freakin' clue," I admitted. "They want to show us something, so let's see what they ..."

Jillian suddenly held a finger to my lips, silencing me instantly. Then, placing the same finger on hers, we squatted low and quietly approached some large rocks that were nearby. The dogs, somehow sensing we were now approaching in stealth, fell silent and followed us.

Then I heard it. Two voices, and they were

coming from nearby. One was male, and the other female. And, from the sounds of it, they both sounded young.

Anxious to see what was going on, I carefully peered around the boulder and studied the scene in front of me. As we had guessed, there were two people down at the water. Both had buckets, and both were holding various pieces of raw seafood in their hands. Out in the water, watching intently, was the raft of otters.

"Zachary!" Jillian quietly whispered in my ear. "Look! The otters are holding more coins! Whoever those two people are, they're trying to get the coins from the otters!"

TEN

The four of us crouched behind the boulders and watched the two people, one man and one woman, unsuccessfully try to relieve the otters of their prized shellfish smashers. The young otter from before, evidently Sherlock's new best friend, was there, holding a coin, and staring impassively at the couple on the beach. The duo continued to throw bits of seafood at the otters, but only succeeded in driving the otters farther from the shore.

"Why isn't this working?" the male demanded. "You said all we had to do was feed the otters. Well, this isn't working, is it?"

I cocked my head. The voice sounded young. Just then, the female turned to reach for the second bucket, affording us a look at her face. She was tall, had her long straight brown hair gathered up in a ponytail, and was slim. Her face had high cheekbones, was riddled with acne, and I caught a glimpse of metal in her mouth. Did that mean...? Yes, she was wearing braces!

"This kid is young," Harry whispered.

"Around fifteen or sixteen," Jillian quietly guessed. "It looks like they're trying to do what we did: bribe the otters with food so that they'll abandon their rocks. The problem is, they're only driving them away."

"How do they even know to do that, man?" Harry whispered.

I looked at Harry and gave him a thumbs up.

"And that is the million dollar question."

"I wonder why it isn't working for them," Julie wondered aloud.

"They're too impatient," I quietly observed. "They have to gain the otters' trust. The raft needs to know they're there to provide food."

"They know something is up," Julie guessed. "That's why none of them have taken any of the food, nor have they dropped any rocks. I counted ten otters who were carrying coins when we arrived. That number is now up to eleven."

"Twelve," Jillian quietly corrected.

"What do you want us to do, man?" Harry wanted to know.

I saw that of the four of us, everyone was holding their cell phones, except for me. The intent was clear. One of us should be calling the police. Unfortunately, Murphy's Law put in its usual appearance and bit us squarely on the rear. Harry's phone chimed just then. Loudly.

"Did you hear that?" the male voice exclaimed. "Somebody is here!"

An angry male face appeared over the rocks and

scowled at us. I placed his age around the same as that of the girl's. These kids were no older than sixteen, tops.

"There's a group of people over here," the boy called. "And they're spying on us!"

And just like that, the boy produced a snub-nosed revolver and pointed it at us.

"Get out here, all of you. Now!"

The girl was staring at us, as though we had pointed ears and were making the Vulcan peace signs with our hands.

"Wh-who are you? What are you doing here?"

I threw a dark look at Harry as we all reluctantly walked around the boulders to confront our adversaries. I pointed at Harry's cell.

"Explain that. Did someone text you just now?"

Harry held up his phone and smiled sheepishly, "Rugby scores. It's the playoffs, man! I get text alerts whenever certain countries play. Hey, man, don't balk at technology. Embrace it!"

"I'm gonna embrace it all right," I vowed.

"Who are you?" the girl asked again.

"We should be asking you the same thing," I stated. I looked at the boy and down at the gun he was holding. "Do you mind? Put that away before someone gets hurt."

"Don't think I know how to use this?" the kid challenged. "I've had plenty of practice with it. My father takes me shooting every other weekend."

"When he has visitation rights?" Harry

guessed.

The gun swung toward Harry.

"Shut up! You don't know anything about me!"

"Other than hitting that nail on the head," I mumbled.

Harry, overhearing, gave me a quick thumbs-up.

"Who are you people?" the boy demanded. "What are you doing here?"

"How did you find us?" the girl added.

"We'll make a deal with you," Jillian calmly began. "You tell us who you are, and we'll tell you who we are. And, we'll even throw in what we're doing here, okay?"

I glanced down at the dogs, surprised they weren't barking their fool heads off. Usually, in these situations, which I'm sorry to say have been happening with an unpleasant increase in frequency, the dogs would be growling, barking, or snarling. But this time? Psssht. This time, the dogs weren't even growling. In fact, looking down at them, I noticed they had settled onto the ground and were watching us, as though we were having a pleasant conversation. Why weren't the little snots barking?

The girl finally nodded. "Fine. My name is Beth. Beth Williams. This is Michael ... er, Mike."

"Does Mike have a last name?" Jillian politely inquired.

"Don't tell them my last name," Mike growled.

"A deal is a deal," Jillian reminded Beth.

"Mike Thompson. He's my boyfriend."

"How old are you, Beth?" Jillian asked.

Beth frowned and waggled a finger. "No, that's not the arrangement. You need to tell me who you are and how you found us."

Jillian nodded. "You're right. You've upheld your end of the deal, so I'll honor mine. My name is Jillian Cooper. That's my boyfriend over there, holding the dogs. His name is Zachary Anderson. Over there, with the beard, is Harrison Watt and standing next to him is his wife, Julie. They're friends of ours. As for what we're doing here, well, we're on vacation."

A loud bark made everyone jump.

Jillian smiled and looked down at Sherlock.

"I'm sorry, boy. I didn't mean to forget you. Beth? Down there, with the orange, black, and white coat is Sherlock. Watson is the other corgi."

Beth smiled fleetingly. "Sherlock and Watson. That's cute."

"What's the matter with you?" Mike snapped. "They're stalling for time! I should just take care of them right now!"

Okay, that ought to earn the kid some barks and growls from the dogs. But, did they? Nope. In fact, it looked as though Sherlock wanted to go over to the two kids and give them a proper introduction.

"What's wrong with you?" I quietly hissed at the dogs. "Why aren't you barking?"

"Smart dogs," Mike coolly returned. "They

know if they act up, they'll get shot."

I frowned. *If you so much as threaten my dogs, you miserable little puke, then I'll ...*

Jillian thumped me in the gut. She must have seen the look on my face and correctly guessed what I had been thinking. I scowled at Mike, but not before looking at Jillian and giving her a reassuring smile. I won't do anything yet, my dear. And I stress the word *yet.*

A thought occurred. I pointed at the nearly empty buckets of seafood.

"How did you learn about what we did here yesterday?" I wanted to know. "I didn't think that was common knowledge."

It was the girl's turn to look surprised.

"Wait, that was you? You're the ones who were able to get the coins from the otters?"

"Beautiful," Mike said, as he brandished his gun. "If you did it before, then you can do it again. Make the otters give us their rocks."

"How do you even know about them?" Julie wanted to know. "Do you have some type of connection to the aquarium?"

"I work there," Beth returned. "Well, I mean, I volunteer there."

"You're the minor," I guessed, as a few pieces of the puzzle clicked into place. "We just heard about you earlier today. You obviously must have been at the aquarium and overheard us, although we certainly didn't see you."

"There were plenty of places to hide in there,"

Harry reminded me. “And, an aquarium that size always has running water, loud pumps, and so forth. You wouldn’t have been able to see her or hear her, bro.”

“How did you know where to find us?” Mike asked, growing angry again. “No one knew we were here.”

I calmly pointed down at the dogs, “They did. We’re here because of them. Whether they heard you or they smelled you, it’s irrelevant. They knew you were here.” Right about then, I stared down at the nearly empty bucket that was closest to me, then out at the water, where the otters were floating, and then back at the girl. “You’re one of Jack Carlton’s volunteers. So, does that mean you’re the one who killed him?”

“He drowned,” Mike spat.

“He drowned, ’cause he had been stung by one of the most venomous octopuses in the world,” I corrected. “The blue-ringed octopus, native to waters much warmer than this.” I then looked at Beth. “But, you already knew that, didn’t you?”

“What’s he talking about?” Mike demanded, as he turned to Beth. “You said that guy drowned. He did drown, right?”

Beth’s eyes teared up. “Yes, he drowned. It was an accident! He wasn’t supposed to die!”

The gun Mike had been holding slowly lowered until it was pointing straight down at the sandy ground.

“Is what they’re saying true? Did you do something to that diver?"

Sensing an opportunity which might buy us some time, or possibly an avenue to escape, I decided to try and get the two youngsters into a full-blown argument. Don't ask me why. It must be my evil streak.

"Your girlfriend stole one of fifteen juvenile, blue-ringed octopuses," I told Mike. I glanced down at the dogs, but they were still supremely uninterested in the tense situation we had found ourselves in. "Somehow, and we don't know how as of yet, she got the thing to sting Mr. Carlton. I don't know how long it took to affect him, but it caused paralysis, which meant he literally stopped moving and, unfortunately, breathing. Because of her," I said, pointing at Beth, "an experienced, well-respected diver lost his life."

By this time, Beth was full-on bawling, letting out great, heaving sobs. Her eyes were squeezed shut and she rocked back and forth. I kinda felt like a jerk, but it was working. For all intents and purposes, Mike was now staring at his girlfriend as though she was a stranger to him. And, for all I knew, maybe that's what Mike was now thinking.

"You admit to being the person who stole that octopus baby?" Jillian softly asked.

Beth's tear-streaked face nodded.

"How did you get it to sting Jack Carlton?" Jillian continued.

"It wasn't supposed to be him!" Beth insisted. "I never wanted to kill him!"

"And yet, you did," I added.

"How did it happen?" Jillian asked.

"I ... I put the octopus in a dive mask," Beth hesitantly began. "It was tiny. I watched it settle inside the nose piece and figured this would be perfect. I thought for certain it would look like an accident."

"Finding a poisonous octopus in a dive mask would certainly raise a question or two," I argued.

"You don't dive, do you?" Beth accused.

I frowned. "Hey, I may not look like it now, but I used to. What does that have to do with anything?"

"If you suddenly felt like you couldn't breathe," Beth said, "then more than likely you'd rip the mask off your face. And if that happens? What then?"

"The octopus would be flushed out to sea," I guessed, drawing a nod from the young girl.

"If you didn't want to kill Jack Carlton," Julie slowly began, "then why put that thing in his mask?"

"It wasn't his mask!" Beth insisted. "Mr. Carlton must have been in a hurry. He grabbed the wrong mask by mistake. I would never hurt him. I care about him."

"You sure have a funny way of showing someone that you care."

"I said I didn't mean to kill him!" Beth raged, all remorse gone.

"If not him," I said, frowning, "then who was

your target?"

"That ... that b-bitch! Sherry!"

"Sherry?" Jillian repeated, puzzled. "Wait. The girl who was found hiding in the bushes the day Jack died."

"This is all her fault!" Beth wailed. "If it wasn't for her, then none of this would've happened."

"You were trying to kill another volunteer?" I incredulously repeated. "Why? What in the world for? You're both volunteers, for crying out loud. You guys aren't even getting paid!"

"Jealousy," Jillian guessed.

Beth nodded. "He doesn't need another female volunteer. He has me! I put in all the long hours. I do all the jobs no one else wants to do. Mr. Carlton doesn't need anyone else but me."

"Didn't I hear somewhere that he had six volunteers?" I said, as I turned to Jillian. "Wouldn't that suggest he has enough work for everyone? Maybe he wants to have all those volunteers."

"But he didn't need them!" Beth wailed, sounding very much like her age. "He had me! Since Mr. Carlton used so many volunteers in his many projects, I had to show him that I was the best."

"Wait," I said, as I held up my hands in a time-out gesture. "Are you suggesting that there was a competition among the volunteers to see who'd become the favorite? What in the world for?"

"You don't understand," Beth accused. "It was a well-known fact that Mr. Carlton was sent all over the world. He always told us volunteers that we really should have passports, 'cause he never knows when he might need help when he leaves the country. As for Sherry, well, he's taken her a few times to South America. To Venezuela, of all places! That should have been me! I want to go to another country!"

"Beth, how old are you?" Jillian suddenly asked.

"I'm sixteen. Why?"

"Do you think it's socially acceptable for a grown man to take an underage girl with him?" Jillian pointedly asked. "To a foreign country, of all places?"

"He could," Beth sniffed, as her nose lifted. "If he wanted to, then he could have made it happen."

"Perhaps," Jillian said, shrugging. "But, it's highly unlikely. You're still a child. You'd have to wait until you became a legal adult."

"Holy crap on a cracker," I said, shaking my head. "She was hoping for something more, wasn't she?"

"Did you think Jack Carlton would develop feelings for you?" Julie asked, acting concerned. "Don't you watch television? A grown man would never fraternize with a young child. And if they did, don't you know how many times it ends badly for the child?"

"Stop calling me a child!" Beth demanded. "I'm smarter than you, more motivated than you …"

"… and will be doing more jail time than Julie ever will," I interrupted. I glanced over at Mike.

"What do you think, pal? Are you still willing to stand beside her?"

"You never said anything about killing a guy," Mike insisted. "You said you knew where we could find some sunken treasure. We were going to collect all these coins and sell them! You even told me you found some buyers online!"

She thought she'd be able to keep the treasure? Drawing on some of my newly acquired info I had gleaned while researching shipwrecks, I smiled. "Did she also tell you that, according to the Abandoned Shipwreck Act of 1987, any sunken ship found within the territorial boundaries of the United States belongs to the United States?"

"Nice one, Zachary," Jillian whispered.

"You made that up," Mike defiantly insisted.

I shook my head. "I really didn't. It has a silly name but, unfortunately for you, that Act really exists. That's why there are so few treasure hunts on American soil. Or in the American water. If you find something, then it automatically belongs to Uncle Sam."

"Oh, this keeps getting better and better!" Mike complained. "Is what he's saying true? We wouldn't be allowed to keep the treasure?"

"The government wouldn't have to know about it," Beth snapped, growing angry and defensive for the first time. "Who was going to tell them? You? I certainly wasn't."

Another random thought occurred. And no, this one wasn't designed to piss either of the teenagers off. What can I say? I have a knack for poking the bear.

"Tell me something," I began. I pointed out at the otters, who were still in the area, but floating a respectable distance from shore. "What did you hope to gain from this? I mean, you guys mentioned you had some buyers lined up for the sunken treasure? You're only a kid, who is still ... wait. Let me guess. You're in high school?"

Beth nodded.

"Right. You're still in school. Do you really want to tangle with people who willingly deal in black market treasure?"

"It was a risk," Beth admitted.

"You found the *San Augustin*, didn't you?" I said.

A look of defiance appeared on the young girl's face, "Maybe. What's it to you? That treasure is mine!"

"That's a lofty goal for someone so young," Harry observed. "What's up with that? What do you plan on doin' with all that money?"

"Say nothing," Mike advised.

"We know you know the location of the wreck," Jillian soothingly told the girl. "What harm could there be in telling us what you plan on doing with the recovered coins? Were you going to use the money to start your whale institute?"

"I was going to prove to Jack Carlton that I could be taken as seriously as any adult," Beth sobbed. "Yes, you're right. I found the location of

San Augustin. How? Not by making multiple dives day after day, month after month, wasting tons of money. I found it by studying, reading. I determined where the wreck went down, I calculated where the currents would have dropped the wreckage, and after all these years, where it would have ended up now. After I obtained my deep water certification, Mike and I went diving. Sure enough, we found it."

"But so did the stupid otters," Mike groused. "Why couldn't they leave well enough alone?"

Ignoring him, Beth continued, "With the coordinates in my hand, I went to see Mr. Carlton. Since I had located the wreck earlier in the year when Mr. Carlton had been in New Zealand, I had to wait for him to return to the aquarium. When I saw he was finally back, I approached him and said I had something he really needed to see. And it was urgent. Sherry sensed something was up. She was jealous of me. She always has been. She knew I had something that Mr. Carlton was going to want to see. So, she kept close to him in an attempt to take credit for whatever I was planning on sharing."

These volunteers were sounding more and more like a bunch of school children. Then again, Beth was still in school. Who knew how many kids volunteered at the aquarium?

"What happened?" I softly asked, already knowing the outcome.

"Once I knew Mr. Carlton was convinced I was serious, and he agreed to go diving with me, we made plans to meet out at the beach. Finally, I was going to get my due. I was finally going to show Mr. Carlton proof I had discovered the long, sought-after *San Augustin*. With any amount of luck, Mr. Carlton would want to film the discovery for National Geographic. It would bring more fame to Mr. Carlton, and he would reward me by taking me under his wing, perhaps introducing me to some of his associates at National Geographic."

"Like a proud papa," I said, throwing enough of a sneer to earn myself a scowl from the boyfriend.

"But, as luck would have it, on the day of the scheduled dive, I overheard Sherry ask Mr. Carlton if she could accompany us. I almost cried when I heard him agree to her request. This was my time! This was my discovery! Why did she have to butt her nose in where it didn't belong? Well, I had to put a stop to her."

"So, you made plans to take Sherry out of the equation," Jillian deduced.

Beth nodded. "Exactly. I stole one of those blue-ringed octopus babies, stashed it in Sherry's mask, and waited to go diving. The only problem was, Mr. Carlton was stuck on a video call with one of his friends in another country. He was late to our meeting, so he ..." At this point, Beth trailed off and started sobbing. Collecting herself, she cleared her throat and started again. "He was late. Because he was late, he was rushed. He grabbed his and Sherry's masks and hurried to the beach, only, in his haste, he took Sherry's mask, by mistake."

"Did Sherry grab his first?" I asked, curious.

Beth shrugged. "I don't know. I wouldn't put it past her. I didn't know anything had gone wrong until ... until I saw Sherry suiting up on the beach and then, suddenly, running away. That's when I turned and saw Mr. Carlton, floating face down in the water. I knew immediately what had happened. Somehow, and I didn't know how, he had donned the mask intended for Sherry."

"Sherry freaks," I guessed, as I continued the train of thought, "and hides in the bushes, not sure what to do."

"Oh, I hate her! She ruined everything!"

"If you would have had your way," I told the petulant girl, "then another girl would be dead, instead of Jack Carlton. Don't you get it? You took another person's life! That's something you're going to have to live with for the rest of your life."

Beth sobbed as she fell silent.

Jillian suddenly cleared her throat, "I have a question. Where is Sherry now? And why didn't she go to the police? She clearly knew Jack Carlton died under mysterious circumstances."

"Who on earth is Sherry?" Mike wanted to know, as he turned to confront his young girlfriend once more. "You mean, she's someone you actually wanted to kill? What is wrong with you?"

"You're not one to talk," I pointed out. "You were pointing that gun at the four of us earlier, and you claimed you'd have the fortitude to pull the trigger."

"You know I do," Mike growled. "Whose gun do you think this is?"

"Your daddy's?" Harry nonchalantly quipped.

"It's mine!" Mike insisted. "I know how to handle a gun. I can and will use it if I have to."

"Did you take care of Sherry, too?" I asked, growing angry.

"I never killed anyone!" Mike insisted.

"But she did," I said, pointing at Beth. "Maybe she killed Sherry, too."

"I wanted to," Beth admitted, as she clenched her hands, "but I couldn't find her. She wasn't at her house and she wasn't answering her phone."

"And why would she?" Harry demanded. "You are trying to kill her, man! I'd be lying low, too, if I knew a nutjob like you was looking for me."

"The witch even had the nerve to blackmail me," Beth continued.

There was no mistaking the venom in the young girl's voice. Here was a girl who truly hated another girl, and for what reason? Social status. Beth wanted to lord it over Sherry, that she was Jack Carlton's number one helper, only, if Jack was like any other sensible person, he'd never allow himself to be alone with a minor.

"You were being blackmailed?" Mike repeated, frowning. Then, his eyes opened in shock. "That's why you wanted to borrow $500 from me? Was it to pay this Sherry person?"

"I was going to pay you back," Beth snapped. "What choice did I have? She threatened to tell the police if I didn't do as she said. As soon as we had those coins, we could pay her off and we'd be done with her."

"Pay up in order to keep quiet," I reflected. "It's one of the oldest tricks in the book, and sadly, it usually doesn't end well. For either party."

Beth hurried over to Mike and tried to take the gun from him.

"Knock it off, Elizabeth! I'm not giving you the gun. I told you, you have no experience with it. I do. I'll be keeping it, thank you very much."

Beth pointed a shaking finger at the four of us. Er, the six of us.

"Then make them show you what they did with the otters," Beth shouted. "We need those coins! If they're seen with those coins, then people will know the *San Augustin* is close!"

"A bunch of people already know about them," I pointed out. Beth's angry red face swiveled until she was staring straight at me. "You work at the aquarium. You haven't overheard any of the conversations?"

"You're lying," Beth insisted.

I shook my head. "In this case, I am not. The director, Jon Hawk, knows. So do a number of the staff. Do you really think you'll be able to keep this under wraps? I personally think it's only a matter of time before the aquarium launches a full scale dive, centered in this area. How long before they find the ship? Not long, if you ask me."

"Well, maybe they will and maybe they won't,"

Beth sneered. “At least, when they find the ship, there won’t be any more treasure on it. It’ll be long gone.”

Remembering a bit more from my recent research into shipwrecks, I laughed derisively and crossed my arms over my chest. “Are you telling me that you think the two of you would be able to move sixty tons of treasure that easily? Me thinks not, Grasshopper.”

“Sixty t-tons?” Mike stammered, as he looked at Beth and waited for her to contradict that statement. When she didn’t, his eyes opened wide. “How are we supposed to move that kind of cargo? My uncle’s boat is nowhere near large enough to handle something that weighs so much.”

“Then we’ll bring it up in small loads,” Beth said, growing angry once more, “and make multiple trips. Stop arguing with me about this, Michael! You said you’d help me, no questions asked, right? Well, I need your help!”

“That’d be aiding and abetting,” I translated, as I looked at Mike. For the record, the kid’s gun was still pointed down.

“I … I don’t know, Elizabeth.”

“Don’t you wuss out on me!” Beth cried.

The teen girl lunged forward, intent on relieving Mike of his gun, only he was ready for just such an attack. He stepped to the side, spun to his left, and stuck out a leg. Beth went down onto the sand, hard.

“How d-dare you!” Beth sputtered, as her face

surfaced and rivulets of sand cascaded off her head. "You don't want to help me? Fine! I'll do this all by myself!"

I made a sweeping gesture with one of my hands, "And what about us? What's your plan? The four of us now know what you've been up to. You've indicated you don't want Mike around anymore. How do you plan on getting out of this?"

As if the universe had been waiting for me to ask that very question, police officers suddenly appeared out of nowhere and swarmed the two teenagers. Within moments, it was over. Mike was relieved of his gun and both the teenagers were ordered—at gunpoint—to lie down on the sandy beach. Beth gasped with surprise and immediately raised her hands in surrender. Her face fell as she wordlessly complied with the orders given by the police. After a few moments, Mike did the same. Then, much to my amusement, both teens began laying on the water works, with Mike being far and away the most charismatic actor.

"This is all her doing!" Mike was insisting. "All she said I had to do was help her bring coins up from some sunken ship. She was going to do the rest. I swear!"

"In his defense," I began, "Mike didn't know anything about the death of Jack Carlton. That was all her doing."

The two teens were quickly cuffed, pulled to their feet, and led away. As for us, we were guided away from the water and led back to our hotel, where a couple of familiar faces were waiting for us. I nodded at Officer Adolphson and her grouchy partner, Officer Lewis. Also present was Jon Hawk and a few other aquarium officials I didn't recognize.

"Mr. Anderson, Ms. Cooper," Jon began, as he caught sight of us coming through the hotel's lobby, "tell me you're okay."

"We're fine," I assured the aquarium director. "We have a couple of questions for you, though."

We were led to a sitting area near the hotel's front desk, where we all took seats. Sherlock and Watson curled up by my feet and watched the proceedings with disinterest. Every couple of minutes or so, the dogs looked longingly back the way we had come. I think both of them would much rather be outside, playing in the water with their otter friends.

"How did you know we were in trouble?" I asked, as Jon took a seat next to mine.

"It's easy. We were already watching that beach. As soon as we saw what was happening, we phoned for the police."

"Why were you watching that beach?" Jillian wanted to know.

Jon laughed and shook his head. "Kids. When will they ever learn that sound carries? Ms. Williams was in such a rush to fill several buckets with otter food that she didn't stop to consider how much noise she was making. Several of our staff reported to me what they saw, and noticing the striking similarities to the experiment I personally instructed you to try with the otters earlier, I knew immediately what she was going to try and do. We watched, we waited, we filmed," Jon said, throwing emphasis on the word, "and when we had what we needed, we notified."

"I don't think we were in any danger," Julie said. "I work at the police department in Pomme Valley. I'm no police officer, but we still have a lot of training. The boy, Mike, was showing no signs of aggression or hostility."

"Let's agree to disagree, Jules," Harry sputtered. "He had a gun. He pointed it at us."

"For only a brief time," I recalled. "Then, for the most part, Mike had it pointed at the ground. And, he refused to let Beth have it, citing lack of experience. That must be why the dogs never barked. They somehow knew we weren't in any danger from those two kids."

Jillian nodded. "That's true. I had forgotten about that. Go easy on him, will you?"

"I'll pass that information on," Jon promised. "Now, about *San Augustin*, did you hear Ms. Williams say she located the wreck?"

The four of us nodded.

"Did she, perhaps, say where it was? Did she give exact coordinates?"

"No," I said, shaking my head. "But, we do know it's not far from where those otters are. They keep pulling coins off the wreck. Apparently, they really enjoy using those sparkling rocks."

"Come Monday," Jon began, "I'll be dispatching several teams of divers to McAbee Beach. If that girl can find a sunken Spanish ship, then so can we. We'll find it, document it, and preserve whatever treasure is left."

"Good for you," I said. "Hey, let me ask you something. Whatever happened to Sherry?"

"She hasn't reported for her duties at the aquarium in the last few days," Jon solemnly reported. "We contacted her employer and discovered she hasn't shown for work there, either. To say we're concerned is an understatement."

"Do you think Beth found her?" Jillian asked.

Jon shrugged. "Officer Adolphson said she personally drove by Sherry's apartment, but her roommate also stated she had been missing."

"I sure do hope she turns up safe and sound," Jillian wistfully said. "I'd hate to think that something happened to her."

I nodded. "You and me both."

"That goes for us, too," Jon said.

The aquarium director then reached into his inside jacket pocket and pulled out four envelopes. He handed one to each of us. Opening my envelope, I could see an ID card and a printed letter with Monterey Bay Aquarium's logo on it. Skimming through the letter, I started smiling. Jon was giving the four of us lifetime memberships to the aquarium. There'd be no more charging us admission whenever we came for a visit.

"Wow," I said, as I placed the ID card and letter

back into its envelope. "I appreciate that. I really do. You didn't have to, but I believe I can speak for the four of us when I say, I'm glad you did."

"It's not often we can reward members of the public for helping our facility," Jon explained. "Consider this our way of saying thanks. Plus, Sherlock and Watson did find the missing dive log. And ... you and Ms. Cooper are helping us with our security issues."

Jillian and I both nodded.

We all stood and shook Jon's hand. After the aquarium's team left, we filled out statements for the police, answered enough questions to be able to write a novel (trust me on this one), and ended up returning to the same seats where we had been sitting before. After all, it had been a harrowing day.

Detecting movement in my peripheral vision, I could see the manager of the hotel waving at me. He was behind the counter and gesturing at a package that had recently been delivered. My eyebrows shot up, my pulse quickened, and suddenly, I found myself out of breath. It was here? Was it Saturday already?

It was time to reveal my surprise.

ELEVEN

"Are you ready to do this?" Harry asked me, using a low voice. He was uncharacteristically serious as he handed me the one item I had asked him to hold on to for the duration of this trip. "You can still change your mind, bro."

"Do you honestly think I should?" I asked, as I dropped my voice and matched his sincerity. "I thought you said I was making the right decision."

"I did," Harry insisted, "and I still do. I'm just worried about you, man. You seem all flustered, like you're nervous."

"Who wouldn't be nervous about something like this?" I stammered. "I never thought I'd be asking another person this particular question. I mean, after I lost Samantha, I would've sworn I'd never feel this way about another woman. It's just ... well, it's ... I mean ..."

Harry placed a reassuring hand on my shoulder. "You have nothing to worry about, man. Jillian is crazy about you. Besides, I think you pulled off this little surprise quite well. Jules doesn't even know what's gonna happen, and you know how much she hates me keeping surprises from her."

"I'm hoping she'll understand this one time."

"She will, bro. She will. Okay, follow me. I know they're sitting near the bar."

"And her parents?"

I followed Harry into the hotel's restaurant and looked around. Harry nudged my shoulder and pointed at an elderly couple sitting nearby, with conveniently placed menus obscuring their faces.

"Oh, that's not obvious at all," I groaned.

"They'll be fine," Harry said.

"Were Vance and Tori able to make it?"

Harry turned and pointed at another table on the other side of the room. I glanced over just in time to see Vance give me a thumbs up. His wife, Tori, was there and smiled warmly at me. Then, I saw Vance glance over at Jillian's table, say something and, just like that, their faces were hidden behind a couple of menus, too. Jillian must have looked their way, but thankfully, didn't see anything out of the ordinary.

"Are you ready for this?"

I opened the ring box. Inside was a platinum tanzanite engagement ring with diamond accents, set in a classic setting. The stone was just over two carats, which if you've ever shopped for those pricey bluish purple stones, you'll know that it wasn't cheap. Both the metal and stones had been polished to a radiant shine. Snapping the box closed, I pocketed it, looked at my friend, and swallowed nervously.

"You bet. Let's do this."

Harry nodded. "Roger that, bro. All right, give me just a few minutes, and I'll get Jules out of the way."

"Thanks, buddy."

Harry then strode up to the table, pulled out his chair, and plunked his butt down.

"Where's Zachary?" Jillian worriedly asked.

"I think he's back there," Harry confided, pointing in the completely opposite direction. "I think he's trying to arrange to secretly pay for tonight's dinner. Little does he know I already took care of it."

"That's awfully sweet of you," Jillian proclaimed, placing a hand over Harry's and giving it a gentle squeeze.

Right then, I arrived. I gave Jillian a quick kiss, knocked fists with Harry when the girls weren't looking, and gave Julie a smile.

"Hey, guys," I began. "I have to be honest here. I'm really starting to enjoy going on vacation with other people. I mean, this trip is gonna be one for the books."

Jillian started ticking off points on her fingers. "It's not often you solve a murder, uncover an illegal treasure hunting operation, solve a stolen coin case, and then become lifelong members of what is probably one of the most famous aquariums in the world."

"I'd like to know what we're all gonna do next year, man," Harry added. "How are we gonna top this one?"

"Excuse me," a British female voice interrupted. "Mrs. Julie Watt?"

We all turned to stare at Julie, who was staring incredulously at the waitress.

"Yes? That's me. What can I do for you?"

The waitress held out a slip of paper.

"I am the general manager of the hotel, Mrs. Watt. I was told I could find you in here. Do you recognize this charge, madam?"

Curious, Julie accepted the slip. She narrowed her eyes as she stared at the amount.

"No, I don't. What's going on? Has someone got ahold of one of my credit cards?"

"If you'll come this way, madam," the British lady was saying, holding out an arm and indicating which direction she needed to go, "then I'm sure we can get to the bottom of this."

"What? Oh, of course. Would you excuse me? I need to find out what's going on here."

Harry also pushed away from the table.

"I'd better go and see what the problem is. Someone is trying to use her personal card? That can't be good, man."

"We'll be fine," I assured our friends as—together—they walked away from the table. Had Jillian been studying Harry's face, then the jig would have been up, since she would have seen him sporting a huge smile.

"I hope everything is all right," Jillian said nervously. "Maybe Harry used the wrong card? What do you think, Zachary? Oh! Wh-what ...?"

When Jillian turned to look back at me, I watched her eyes widen with surprise as she saw me down on one knee, with the ring box open and held out to her.

"Jillian," I hesitantly began, "I never thought I'd be in this position again. Uh, literally. I was always under the impression that lightning just wasn't capable of striking the same person twice. Yet, it happened. To me. And, I like to believe, to you as well. So, here we are, in Monterey, California, and I have a question for you."

I saw Jillian's mouth open, as if to say something, but nothing came out.

"Jillian Leigh Cooper, will you marry me?"

Jillian's mouth opened again, but as before, nothing was heard. With her eyes open wide, she frantically looked at the table and reached for her water. Finding it low, I slid my glass over to her.

"You're ... I ... oh, my. I can't seem to speak!"

"While I would ordinarily take that as a good sign," I said, as I grinned at my girlfriend, "I kinda need an answer here."

Jillian slid her chair back from the table and rose to her feet. The moment she did, she threw her arms around me and hugged me tight.

"Of course I'll marry you! I love you, Zachary! I think I've loved you from the moment I first saw you in my store!"

Grinning like a love-struck teenager, I pulled the ring from its box and slid it on Jillian's left hand.

"Oh, it's beautiful," Jillian whispered, as she held her hand this way and that, so she could admire the ring from every direction. "And is that tanzanite?"

I nodded. "Yep. I know it is your favorite."

Jillian hugged me again. She started to sit back down when she saw Harry and Julie coming toward us. Harry was holding a bottle of champagne. A very expensive bottle of champagne, Crystal Rose. I had special-ordered a bottle of Jillian's exquisite champagne and it had been delivered earlier today. I figured if I didn't chicken out then it'd be the perfect way to celebrate.

Harry was all smiles. "Congrats, you two! Seriously, bro, it couldn't happen to a nicer dude. I know you two will be very happy!"

Jillian turned to look back at the direction Harry and Julie had just come from. There, walking toward her, holding a tray of crystal flutes and the second bottle of Crystal Rose I had later added to my order, was my second confidante, namely the British lady from before. I only knew her as Maggie H., and that was because it was on her nametag.

I pointed at the second bottle of bubbly. "That's a good idea. I'm thinking we're all going to need it."

"I have two other bottles in reserve," Maggie confided. "When you've hosted as many events as I have, you get a feeling for how many bottles of champagne are needed for a party this size."

I shrugged. "If you say so. Just leave me the ..."

"It's already taken care of," Maggie assured me. "Compliments of the MPD."

"I'm definitely going to have to send them a case or two of wine," I mumbled to myself.

"A party this size?" Jillian repeated. "Excuse me, Maggie is it? What did you mean by that?"

Maggie smiled, and then turned away.

"What's going on?" Jillian suspiciously asked, as she turned to look at me. I grinned at her and shrugged. Jillian then looked over at Julie. "Is everything okay with you and Harry?"

"It was, just as soon as he explained what Zack was about to do," Julie confided. She and Jillian embraced. "I'm so happy for you. No one deserves to be happy more than you and Zack."

Maggie set the tray of flutes on the table and began pouring champagne. Also at that time, a group of four waiters and waitresses appeared, and rapidly slid several other tables next to ours, effectively increasing our seating by eight. Jillian turned to me and pointed at the tables.

"I don't understand. 'A party this size?' Additional tables? Is someone else joining us?"

I nodded. "I couldn't ask you to marry me without asking your dad first. And, they asked if they could be included."

"You talked to my parents? Where? When? They've been gone to ..." Jillian trailed off as a shocked smile appeared on her face. "Oh my gosh!

Is that why they said they were coming back early? Did you arrange this?"

I pointed at a table three spaces away. Jillian gasped as she recognized the faces of her parents, who slowly rose to their feet. Her mother, a kind, caring woman in her mid-seventies, pulled her daughter in for a hug.

"Mom?" Jillian squeaked out, between sobs. "What are you doing here? How long have you known Zachary was going to do this?"

"About three months now," Jillian's father answered, as he stepped forward to pull her in for a hug. Wyatt Cooper was a stern-looking, older gentleman in his late seventies. "Zack called me up out of the blue, asked permission to marry you, which I heartily gave, mind you, and wanted to know if we'd like to witness the proposal, here in California. Who was I to turn that down? We cut our trip short and hurried home."

Jillian held up her hands in a time-out. "Wait. Just wait a moment. Are you saying you've been back for over two months?"

"And it's been very hard not telling you anything," her mother, Clara, said. "I don't like keeping secrets from anyone, but for this? I could see fit to bend my own rules."

Wyatt approached me and held out a hand, which I immediately took. The older man's handshake was firm and resolute. He looked me in the eye and nodded.

"I'm happy for you two. And, if I'm allowed to

say this ... it's about time. What took you so long, you knucklehead?"

"Dad!" Jillian cried, embarrassed.

"Oh, I'm just teasing the boy," Wyatt assured her, giving me a wink.

Jillian placed a hand on her head and immediately sat down. "Oh, my head is spinning. This is almost too much to take in at the same time. I ... now I know I'm losing it. Those two look like Vance and Tori. They ... Zachary Michael, you didn't!"

We all turned to see my detective friend, Vance Samuelson, and his wife, Tori, approach the table. They were both grinning. More handshakes ensued, and more tears were shed.

"I cannot believe Zachary had the fortitude to pull this off without me knowing anything about it!" Jillian exclaimed, as she looked around the large table filled with our family and friends. "I'm surprised you didn't invite your parents to come up here. I would have liked to see them again."

I grinned and jammed my hands into my pants pockets. "Who says I didn't?"

Right on cue, two more people approached the table and slid out chairs. Jillian gasped again as she looked into the smiling faces of my father, William Anderson, and my mother, Dana.

"Were you hiding somewhere in here, too?" Jillian mock-accused.

My father grinned and pointed at the other end of the restaurant.

"We saw it all, my dear. Zachary, we're proud of you."

I wasn't sure how I was supposed to take that, since I wasn't a child anymore. Smile and nod? Sure, that ought to work.

"Umm, thanks," I said, as I nodded. "To be honest, I've been wanting to ask that question for a while now."

"You have?" Jillian repeated, amazed.

"You have?" Vance echoed.

I shrugged. "Of course. Once I realized I was open to the idea of getting married again, it was all I could seem to think about. So, I figured this setting would be perfect, thus allowing everyone to relax and enjoy the sun, beach, and water."

"But we're leaving tomorrow!" Jillian protested.

"Are we?" I slyly asked. "We've pretty much worked during our whole vacation. I already arranged it with the hotel. We'll be leaving in four more days. That is, if you're amenable to spending more time here with me."

"Absolutely!" Jillian exclaimed. She drew me in for a kiss, which earned us some hoots and hollers from our friends. "What did you have in mind?"

"Well, I thought we could take our first set of scuba lessons here."

"Wait, I thought we were all gonna try to lose some weight first," Harry protested.

"You can if you want to," I told my friend. "However, I should also inform you that ... how do

I put this? Muscles weigh much more than …"

"… fat?" Harry finished for me. "Is that what you were gonna say, bro?"

"Harry, I'm trying to tell you that, right now, you have the advantage. Don't you remember our swim test? We had to tread water for at least fifteen minutes. Both of us had a very difficult time with that."

"True," Harry slowly admitted. "I don't know, man. This is kinda sudden."

"Did I mention that the aquarium is not only picking up the tab, but will also be loaning us the equipment? We don't even have to rent anything."

"What are you guys talking about?" Vance wanted to know.

"Zachary and Harry already have their open water certification," Jillian explained. "Julie and I don't. We were going to get certified so we could dive together."

"Dude, you're a diver?" Vance asked me, impressed. "I didn't know."

I grinned. "Hey, I'm versatile. What about you, pal? Want to take the class with us? Do you think your mom could watch your girls for another couple of days?"

Tori triumphantly held up her phone. "I already asked, and yes. The answer is yes. How exciting! I've always wanted to go scuba diving!"

"There's one other thing I ought to tell you," I said, as I looked at my group of family and friends. "The scuba lessons? They're being held in the aquarium, in one of the tanks."

"Oooo, count me in!" Tori exclaimed. "Vance, what do you say?"

"Sure, why not? Sounds like fun!"

I looked over at my parents. "Mom, Dad, I assume you're heading back to Phoenix?"

My parents both nodded. "But not until tomorrow," my mother added.

"Good. We would like to show you around, starting with a new playmate we discovered for the dogs."

"Where are Sherlock and Watson?" my father wanted to know.

"They're in the room. I took them for an extra-long walk, so both of them should be sound asleep. I was planning on stopping by to pick them up in a little bit."

"Bring towels," Jillian reminded me. "Don't forget to grab some towels."

"And towels," I sighed. "Dogs. There's never a dull moment."

"So when are you going to tell us what you've been up to?" Vance inquired, as he took the bottle of beer that was just placed before him and took a healthy swig. "From what I hear, you four have been having the time of your lives!"

Harry, Julie, Jillian, and I shared a conspiratorial look before bursting with laughter. I nodded, raised my own beer, and took a drink.

"What's so funny?" my detective friend wanted to know.

"Dude, I have no idea where to begin."

Tori clapped her hands and settled back in her chair. "Oooo, I do like a long story. Especially when you're telling it, Zack."

Vance's smile melted off his face and he frowned at his wife.

"Really, Tor? Must you bring that up here?"

"Bring what up here?" my mother wanted to know.

"Since you let it slip about what type of books I write," I began, as I smiled at my mom, "all of my friends have taken the liberty of seeing how well I write. Tori was already a fan."

"I looooove his stories!" Tori confirmed, winking at her husband.

"I feel like you're hitting on my wife whenever she does that," Vance grumbled, which caused me to nearly choke on my beer.

"I'm doing no such thing!" I protested.

Tori reached across the table and laid her hand over mine. "Don't you let him bother you. He's just teasing, aren't you? Vance?"

"Yeah, sure. Jerk."

Thankfully, he had a grin on his face when he said that, which caused the rest of the table to erupt with laughter.

"Let's see," I said, after I took another pull from my bottle. "This vacation started with us discovering a dead body."

Vance's attention was suddenly focused entirely on me.

"You're kidding."

I shook my head. "Nope. He was a diver. We found him floating not far from here, in McAbee Bay."

For the next thirty minutes, Jillian and I took turns regaling our friends and family with what we had been doing since arriving in Monterey several days ago. Vance couldn't believe that the corgis were able to add yet another murder to their expanding list of solved cases. Remembering something the Monterey police captain had recently told me, I grinned and turned to Harry.

"Hey, that reminds me about something. Remember the wager?"

"What wager?" Vance wanted to know.

"With the local police," Jillian added, as she smiled up at me. She knew full well where I was going with this.

"Right. The local police," I explained, "having heard of the dogs' exploits, challenged them to find a coin stolen from a local collector. Well, seeing how we didn't find that specific coin, well ..."

"Oh, man," Harrison moaned, after I trailed off. "Are you tellin' me we gotta pay for our rooms after all?"

Jillian slowly nodded. "Well, if you want to get technical, it *does* makes sense. Sherlock and Watson found a coin, yes, but it wasn't Chet's coin after all. It was just another one which happened to be minted in the same year, wasn't it?"

I nodded. "It was. It was just dumb luck the

coin that otter was using just so happened to be an exact match to the one we were supposed to find."

"Chet analyzed the deposits on the coin," Jillian recalled. "He told us that particular coin has been in the water for a minimum of two hundred years. There was simply no way that coin could have been taken from his display case only eight months ago."

"Maaaaaann," Harry grumbled.

Julie grinned and placed her hand over her husband's. "You know they're messing with you, don't you?"

Harry's head snapped up. "What? What's that? We don't have to pay the bill after all?"

"The bill has already been paid," I reminded my friend. "Both Jillian and I argued the point with Captain Owens, but he wouldn't hear of it. Since the corgis did find a coin, and helped solve Jack's murder, he said the bet was as good as won. He wouldn't take no for an answer."

Harry glared at me for a few moments before he finally smiled. "Dude, not cool, bro. You had me going."

"Who *did* steal that coin?" Wyatt asked. "Did you ever find out?"

I nodded. "We did. We met him yesterday, unfortunately. He was the son of the guy who installed Chet's security system. His girlfriend was the one who snuck the killer octopus into the mask."

"Whatever happened to the other girl?" Julie

asked. "Did she ever turn up? I'd like to know if she's okay."

Shrugging, I sat back in my chair. "Sherry? She's safe. She was actually hiding out at her brother's apartment. She knew Beth was on to her, and wisely decided to lay low for a few days. Once she found out Beth had been arrested, she contacted the police and told them what she knew."

"Was she really blackmailing Beth?" Jillian wanted to know.

I held up my hands. "I honestly have no idea. The only word we have is Beth's, and based on her behavior and her past history, I'm going to go on record and say I don't trust anything coming out of her mouth."

Jillian smiled at me. "Agreed."

"This girl," Vance began. "Beth, is it? How old is she?"

"Sixteen," I answered.

"A sixteen-year-old convicted felon," Vance said, shaking his head. "That's just sad, if you ask me."

"Poor girl," Jillian lamented.

My father suddenly picked up his glass of wine and held it high.

"A toast. To my son and his future bride."

Everyone rose to their feet. I felt my face flush with embarrassment. Jillian slipped her arm through mine and leaned into me, resting her head on my shoulder.

"We didn't think we'd ever see you this happy

again, son, and it warms our hearts. Jillian? Take good care of him. I believe I can speak for everyone here when I say ... sorry. He's your problem now."

Laughing, everyone clinked glasses together and congratulated the two of us. Looking around at our circle of friends and family, I could only shake my head with amazement. I didn't know how it was possible that I lucked out and found two beautiful women in one lifetime. I don't know what I did to deserve Jillian, but I certainly planned on spending the rest of my life making sure she stayed by my side.

AUTHOR'S NOTE

Anyone familiar with Monterey, CA, and the world-famous Monterey Bay Aquarium, is going to notice right away that I took some liberties with its design, exhibits, and policies. I tried to stay as accurate as I could, but since I am the author, I felt I could bend a few things to make it fit my needs. Plus, I have nearly 7 years of experience working in a zoo, both in maintenance and animal husbandry. It was fun to dust some of that knowledge off and introduce it into the books, but by all means, just know that this is all fiction. Yes, characters and experiences are based on people that I knew back from my zoo days, but in no way should it be inferred that these people are real. It's all fiction.

The *San Augustin* is, in fact, a real ship, and it really did pull in to port at Monterey waaayyy back in the day. And, it did sink and, at present, still hasn't been located. Could it actually be somewhere near Monterey? Technically speaking, it was possible, only highly unlikely. I did mention in the book that the wreck was believed to be about 170 miles farther north than I put it, but again, it's all fiction, so I moved the wreck a wee bit closer. Plus, the actual years of the wreck is believed to be 1595, not 1735, so again, I took a few liberties. Please don't be mad. :) I hope you enjoyed the story!

Finally, I'd like to ask a favor of anyone who has enjoyed the story. If you'd like to know what you can do to help out an indie author, such as myself, then it would have to be leaving a review. Believe it or not, all the book retailers use algorithms to study which books are trending, which are gaining positive reviews, and so forth. Every time you leave a review for a book, you help that author become more 'visible' in the eyes of the search algorithms. You know, something like... "If you like this, then may we recommend that?" Trust me, it really does help.

And lastly, if you'd like to be notified whenever I release a new book, whether it's the latest Corgi Case Files adventure, or something new, like the new Dragons of Andela, you can sign up for my newsletter on my blog, located below.

Happy reading!
J.
November, 2019

WHAT'S NEXT FOR ZACK AND THE CORGIS?

A U.S. Marshal puts in an appearance in Pomme Valley, Oregon, searching for a fugitive rumored to be hiding in the area.

Meanwhile, getting ready to celebrate his milestone 40th birthday, Detective Vance Samuelson manages to convince his friends, Zack Anderson and Harry Watt, to join an adventure-seeking thrill club, the Dysfunctional Daredevils, in an effort to prove they're all still young at heart. And, as luck would have it, the US Marshal believes his missing fugitive just might be among the Daredevils, hiding in plain sight.

Can Zack and the dogs uncover the identity of the disguised murderer? Will any more accidents befall the hapless adrenaline junkies of Pomme Valley? Everyone's favorite canine mystery-solving duo, Sherlock and Watson are on the case!

Sign up for Jeffrey's newsletter to get all the latest corgi news—
Click here

The Corgi Case Files Series
Available in e-book and paperback
Case of the One-Eyed Tiger
Case of the Fleet-Footed Mummy
Case of the Holiday Hijinks
Case of the Pilfered Pooches
Case of the Muffin Murders
Case of the Chatty Roadrunner
Case of the Highland House Haunting
Case of the Ostentatious Otters
Case of the Dysfunctional Daredevils
Case of the Abandoned Bones
Case of the Great Cranberry Caper

Made in United States
Orlando, FL
20 January 2022